To: April B.

Marshmallow Muscles,
Banana
Brainstorms

Sincerely yours:

Jaymin

D0391820

Other Apple paperbacks
you will enjoy:

The Zucchini Warriors
by Gordon Korman

Scared Silly
by Eth Clifford

The Secret Life of Dilly McBean
by Dorothy Haas

Sixth Grade Secrets
by Louis Sachar

Just Tell Me When We're Dead!
by Eth Clifford

Marshmallow Muscles, Banana Brainstorms

Karen T. Taha

AN
APPLE
PAPERBACK

SCHOLASTIC INC.
New York Toronto London Auckland Sydney

ISBN 0-590-43394-6

12 11 10 9 8 7 6 5 4 3 2   0 1 2 3 4 5/9

Printed in the U.S.A.   40

First Scholastic printing, June 1990

To Tarek
This one was always for you.

Chapter 1

"Well, Pitt, m' boy, what will you go out for this year? Football? Baseball? Track?" Uncle Harley leaned back and tugged on his gold watch chain. He hooked one thumb in the pocket of his green plaid vest and played a drum roll on his solid belly. Mom and Dad smiled expectantly.

Here it comes again, I thought. I should have been prepared, since the same question came up every September 2nd, which not only marks the first week of school, but also happens to be my birthday.

I looked down at my scrawny 5'10" frame anchored by size 13 feet. "I don't think I'm good enough, Uncle Harley," I mumbled to the table, hating the hot red flush rising up my neck.

"Not good enough?" Uncle Harley's eyebrows quivered like nervous caterpillars.

"Well"—I studied the guaranteed biodegradable, no-artificial-colors, brown-paper plate in front of me—"in football, I'm known as Marshmallow Muscles. Last summer the baseball coach told me to take up soccer. And when I went out for basketball, I ended up dribbling the ball on my toes." I looked at my parents. "Let's face it. I'm never going to be an athlete like you."

"Nonsense!" Uncle Harley exploded. "The son of Tom and Judith Kowalski doesn't just give up. Look at your parents' medals."

Uncle Harley marched to the trophy case that covered one whole wall of our living room. The trailer jiggled with each step of his 200 aged but well-muscled pounds. "Don't forget your father finished third in the Detroit Decathlon, m' boy! Why, if he hadn't been overcome by air pollution, he would've won." Dad flexed his biceps modestly.

"And your mother! *Judith Kowalski, Women's Champion Weight Lifter, Detroit, 1968,*" he read from the biggest trophy. "Someone must carry on the Kowalski name, son. With such parents, you're Olympic material. I can see it now—Pitt Kowalski, Olympic Gold Medal Winner!"

He jabbed a thick finger at a framed photo in the trophy case. "Jim Bob would be so proud of you!"

"That reminds me," said Dad. He pulled an envelope from his pocket and tossed it to me. "Birthday greetings from our old friends in Detroit."

Inside I found a card and a note. The card was plain white and had a businesslike message—*Best Wishes and Good Health from Henrietta's Health Food Store.* On the back was a recipe for "Best Bran Biscuits this side of Bombay."

The note was from Jim Bob.

Hey, Pitt, hope you enjoy your fourteenth! Here's a little something to help you celebrate. Best wishes, Jim Bob.

He had enclosed a ten-dollar bill and a photograph of himself lifting a huge barbell over his head.

A familiar tightness closed around my throat as I looked at the mounds of muscle straining under Jim Bob's freckled skin. He had a reason for that big smile. If only I was good at something . . . anything! If I wasn't such a *marshmallow*. That's all I was—a first-class, supercolossal *marshmallow!*

My best friend, Alex, fits better into this family than I do, I thought. He was on every team at school—football, basketball, track, soccer—you name it. And the fringe benefits of being a jock weren't too bad either. Alex and Linda Simmons had been together since seventh grade, star quarterback and head cheerleader—the perfect couple.

The only girl I ever saw outside of school was Becky Rivera, and that was because she lived in the next trailer and wasn't bad at shooting baskets. In fact, she beat me most of the time.

Becky Rivera had been the number-one pest in Heaven Hill Trailer Park for as long as I could remember.

When she was three, she cut my hair with the kitchen scissors. Dad called me his little Mohawk for two months.

Another time, when Becky was six, she fell off the teeter-totter and made me swallow my loose tooth. (I was on the other end.) I didn't really dislike Becky. Let's just say that when she came around, trouble wasn't far behind.

I forgave her for everything though when she knocked on the back door with her tennis racquet and interrupted Uncle Harley's next prediction about my glorious athletic future.

"Hi, Marshmallow Muscles! Happy Birthday!" It occurred to me that she hadn't stopped smiling since she got her braces off last month. She handed me a small package, no bigger than a Hershey bar, wrapped in blue-and-silver foil. "Don't open this in front of your mom," she warned under her breath.

I stuffed the package in my back pocket and ushered her to the dining-room table, where Uncle Harley and Dad were happily contemplating a khaki-brown cake fringed with unsweetened coconut and fourteen parsley-colored candles.

"Be with you in a minute!" Mom called from the bedroom. "Go ahead and light the candles!" She must have decided to finish her last set of daily push-ups.

Licking his lips, Uncle Harley struck a match and began to light the circle of candles. Mom came in panting, wiped her hands on her shorts, and plopped into a chair between my father and Uncle Harley. In her bright yellow T-shirt, and with her long brown ponytail over one shoulder, she didn't look much older than Becky.

"Sit down, Becky," I said.

Becky glared at me. "I *am* sitting down, Pitt Kowalski, and you know it!"

Becky is a little sensitive about how short she is. She pushed her glasses up with one index finger, but her small, perfectly straight nose was simply not nose enough to hold them. They slid down again, and Becky's big brown eyes peered over the rims at me.

Though I blew with all my might, it took two tries to get all fourteen candles out. They left fourteen little green puddles of wax on the brown ripples of icing.

"Well, it finally came, Pitt, m' boy. Your age has passed your shoe size!" Uncle Harley clicked his false teeth and threw a handful of dollar bills into the air.

Becky's eyes widened in surprise, but I shook my head. I had learned a long time ago not to dive for the dollars, because Uncle Harley always picks them up and puts them back in his pocket. Besides, they probably weren't real, just the fake money he sometimes made in his print shop to play jokes with.

Uncle Harley was actually my great-uncle, since he was Dad's uncle. He had been fullback for the Detroit Lions until he hurt his knee. Then he became a model for Sears' catalogs. When Dad's parents were killed in a plane crash, Uncle Harley became a bachelor father, too. I guess he's always been part of our family, or maybe we're part of his. Anyway, he and my parents stick together on most everything, especially sports. If you're a Kowalski, you go for the gold.

Dad patted me on the back so hard I sputtered cranberry juice down my shirt. "And this year you'll be moving up to high school!" That didn't mean much at Desert Hills actually, since the middle school and the high school shared the same building.

Mom looked at me with dreamy eyes. "High school," she sighed. "Oh, to be a teenager again." I believe Mom's idea of paradise would be lifetime retention in high school. Not many girls had managed to be captain of the basketball team, anchor of the relay team, and head cheerleader all at the same time.

"What're you waitin' for, Pitt, m' boy?" asked Uncle Harley, who was sitting back in his chair after picking up his dollars. "Let's get after that cake!" He clicked his dentures to "Happy Birthday to You," one of the many songs he can play on his teeth.

To tell the truth, I wasn't looking forward to the cake. It was Mom's specialty—Wheat Germ Delight with Carob Icing.

"Jim Bob's favorite," she reminded me. "When we lived in Detroit, I made it for him all the time."

"Great! [click, click, click]," said Uncle Harley.

"M-m-m-m," Dad said as he tasted his first bite. "Too bad Jim Bob isn't here now."

I agreed. I would have been happy to let him have my piece.

"Very good, Mrs. Kowalski," Becky murmured, showing off her perfect white smile.

I kicked her under the table, just to let her know I was on to her act.

"Thank you, Becky," Mom said, beaming. "The recipe comes from Henrietta's Health Food Store in Detroit. That lady taught me all I know about cooking healthy food." Poor Henrietta wasn't there to defend herself.

Mom looked at me, and I flashed my braces at her in what I hoped passed for a smile. I quickly stuffed a bit of the grainy stuff into my mouth, gulped some cranberry juice to wash it down, and nodded my approval. If only Mom's "good-for-you" foods could taste good.

I could hardly wait until Sunday. Alex had promised to buy me a chocolate shake for my birthday. In my house, eating chocolate was as bad as smoking cigarettes. And while I wasn't tempted to smoke, a chocolate milk shake was something I couldn't resist. My mouth started to water just thinking about it.

"Thank you for inviting me, Mrs. Kowalski," Becky said, kicking me back before getting up. "I have to run to tennis practice now. . . . I sure enjoyed the cake." She threw me her perfect white smile. "Happy Birthday, Marshm. . . . I mean Pitt."

I noticed she left a good four bites of cake on **her**

plate. If she enjoyed it so much, why didn't she finish it? "Bye, Becky," I answered. "And . . . thanks." I patted my back pocket.

As Becky flew out the door, tennis racquet in one hand and the other holding her glasses in place, I felt my pocket again, more carefully. Yes, something was definitely oozing out of the package and through my jeans. I excused myself and backed out of the kitchen before the scrumptious aroma of Hershey chocolate reached my mother's nostrils. Becky had done it again.

Chapter 2

"Hey, man, why're you so quiet?" asked Alex as I studied my double-chocolate milk shake at Sarah's Ice Cream Parlor Sunday afternoon. He licked the pink foam off the top of his cherry soda. "This is your birthday present. You're supposed to be happy."

I sucked on my straw and held the cold, sweet chocolate in my mouth a moment before I swallowed. "Sorry, Alex. The shake is great. I've just been thinking about how I'm getting older, but I'm not getting better."

Alex threw back his head and laughed. "Man, you sound like a commercial!"

"But it's true," I insisted. "I'm fourteen years old and what do I have to show for it? My parents think I'm a wimp. So does Uncle Harley."

Alex's face turned serious. "Look, Pitt. I don't think you've ever tried hard enough. You just give up when the going gets rough. You need to set some goals, like my father always tells me. Of course, his idea of goals and mine aren't usually the same."

The door jangled, and three girls in T-shirts and rainbow-striped sun visors giggled their way to the counter.

"Hi, Alex!" they chorused, ignoring me as they passed our table.

Alex blushed. "Hi," he mumbled.

"There are three goals *you've* reached."

"I don't even know them!" protested Alex.

"That's the point. You don't know them, but they know you."

Alex reddened even more. "I'm just glad Linda's not around."

The giggling girls carried their marshmallow-chocolate sundaes to a corner, strategically placed so they could admire Alex's left dimple while they ate.

"Look," I began. "You're my best friend, so I can be honest with you. I'd rather have three girls I don't know say hello to me than one Becky Rivera eat my birthday cake.

"I mean, what do you have that I don't have? You're tall, dark, and handsome. . . . I'm tall. . . . So much for that. You're fast on your feet and can handle a football. . . . I have a hard time handling my feet. Strange girls stop to talk to you. . . . My tongue becomes a stranger when I try to talk to girls. . . . I guess we're not so different after all."

Alex closed his eyes. "Let's go, Pitt. Your mom must be right . . . chocolate isn't good for the brain."

The door jangled again. "Probably more of your fan club," I said, turning around.

It was a girl, all right. My milk shake churned to chocolate butter as my stomach did flip-flops. One unbelievably gorgeous girl!

She had honey-blond hair hanging halfway down her back, an upturned nose, and big blue eyes she kept blinking as if the light was too bright.

"I won't be a minute, Daddy!" she called over her shoulder.

"Wow," breathed Alex softly as she walked past our table.

"Double wow," I agreed. "She must be new around here. Did you hear that drawl? I bet she's from the Deep South."

Alex grinned. "Why don't you be the welcome committee, Pitt? You know, make her feel at home."

"Oh, no, not me! She's dream stuff, not real stuff. To make it with that type, you have to be student body president, or Alex Corona, Touchdown King. I'm neither one."

"See what I mean?" said Alex, slurping the last of his soda. "You give up without even trying."

"I'd like a quart of French vanilla, please," said the dream girl, blinking at the soda jerk. She paid for her ice cream and went out as quickly as she had come in.

"Let's go," I said, sliding back my chair.

The last thing I heard as the door closed behind us was a chorus of "Bye, Alex!" coming from the corner table. It was enough to make me toss my cookies . . . milk shake, I mean.

We got outside in time to see a shiny black Mercedes pull away from the curb.

"Alex," I announced as we got on our bikes,

"you're right. I'm setting my goals right now. I'm tired of being wallpaper."

"Did one of your goals just leave in a black Mercedes?" asked Alex.

Determination ran up my spine like a steel rod. "Why not? Anyway, maybe Uncle Harley's right. Maybe I am Olympic material. I just need to find the right sport. I'm gonna try them all till I find the one for me."

"Great!" said Alex. "But don't forget to study your math, so you can help me. My goal this semester is to pass."

"Fine. You help me with football, I'll help you with math."

He left me at the corner of Heaven Hill Trailer Park. "Hope you have time between dates with those girls who'll be falling all over you!" he yelled as he pedaled off.

At the dinner table that night I nonchalantly let my comment drop into the conversation. "Think I'll go out for sports this year, Uncle Harley, but I need to get in shape."

Mom and Dad beamed like a pair of headlights. Uncle Harley smiled so wide I was sure his upper plate would fall into the cabbage soufflé. "Just leave that to me," he said. "We'll build up those marshmallow muscles in no time at all. We start tomorrow!"

Chapter 3

The next day Uncle Harley pushed my bed against the wall and rolled out the exercise mat in front of the full length mirror on the door.

"Okay, Pitt m' boy. Look at yourself," he ordered. "What d'you see?"

What I saw was a mop of brown hair that needed cutting, a pug nose too wide for a skinny face, and a heavy-metal mouth.

"I'll tell you," Uncle Harley continued. "You see flat tire biceps, scarecrow shoulders, and nonexistent pectorals. That's all gonna change."

He dedicated himself to my training every night. "Five more push-ups, Pitt, m' boy. Come on, four more. That's the way. Keep it up! Don't stop! You'll never build those marshmallow muscles that way. Work, Pitt, work! You're gonna be just like Jim Bob."

"Jim Bob!" I collapsed on the floor. "How could I ever be like Jim Bob?"

Uncle Harley rubbed a beefy hand over his scalp and laughed. "Why, he was as skinny as a plucked chicken when we met him—just like you, Pitt, m' boy."

"Come on, Uncle Harley," I panted. "Jim Bob is as strong as a locomotive."

"Determination and hard work," said Uncle Harley. "Ask your mother."

He shook his head, remembering, then fixed his sharp blue eyes on my heaving chest—what there was of it. "Come on, boy. Snap to! Hook your toes under this chair and do twenty sit-ups for me."

Dad was after me every morning. "Outta bed, Pitt. Warm up! You need to run a mile or two before breakfast."

There was nothing more discouraging than prying one eye open and seeing Dad, square jaw set in an energetic smile, hairy chest bobbing up and down, as he jogged in place by my bed.

"Let's go!" he shouted enthusiastically as I staggered down the trailer steps behind him into the chilly desert dawn. I was glad *one* of us was having fun.

"Hello, Mr. Jordan!" Dad called out as we jogged past my band director, or I should say my ex-band director, since I dropped trombone. He was being tugged down the street by a Great Dane who was frantically sniffing every palm tree along the way.

"Whoa, Willy!" Mr. Jordan sat down heavily on the curb. "Mornin', Tom. Mornin', Pitt." He slipped Willy's leash around his wrist, pulled out a pocket mirror and inspected his long, white mustache.

Mr. Jordan had been the band director at Desert

Hills Middle School and High School for as long as I could remember. Last year he gave me extra trombone lessons—for the sake of the band, he said. That's one reason I felt sort of guilty about dropping out. But if I was going to become a legend in the sports world, some sacrifices had to be made.

Mr. Jordan barely had time to drop the mirror in his pocket before Willy jerked him from his resting place.

"Speed up, Pitt," Dad called as Willy's hot breath warmed my backside. "Come on, Pitt! If Jim Bob could do it, so can you!"

Jim Bob again! I couldn't believe he was ever anything but a red-headed mountain of muscle.

"Why does everyone keep talking about Jim Bob?" I asked Mom that afternoon as she carefully eased a spinach loaf into the oven. "What does he have to do with me?"

Mom swiped at the stove with a dishrag and poured me a tall, frosty glass of carrot juice before she sat down. "Well, Pitt, I guess Jim Bob's the main reason we're here in Arizona right now . . . he and Henrietta."

I remembered Henrietta's visit last Christmas. She looked like somebody's grandmother, except she bench-pressed 100 pounds as a warm-up every night.

Mom took a sip of my carrot juice. "Our gym was

above Henrietta's Health Food Store, and that's how we got most of our customers. Not Jim Bob, though. I'm still not sure how he found us."

"Hello, there!" boomed a familiar voice from the back door. The trailer floor creaked as Uncle Harley sauntered into the kitchen. He mopped his face with a large white handkerchief and sank into the nearest chair. "Blamed hot out there," he muttered. "Darndest place I've ever seen. We should've stayed in Detroit."

Mom smiled. "Uncle Harley, maybe you wouldn't be so hot if you didn't wear those three-piece suits."

But Uncle Harley fixed her with a disapproving gaze that dropped to her shorts and bare feet. "Just because we left civilization back in Detroit doesn't mean we should dress like savages, Judith."

Laughing, Mom poured him some carrot juice and handed me a stack of plates from the cupboard. "Set the table and call your father to eat. I'll let Uncle Harley tell you about Jim Bob Smiley."

Uncle Harley loved to tell stories almost as much as he loved sports. So over dinner I learned about Jim Bob's beginnings.

"See, Pitt," Uncle Harley began, "our gym in Detroit was not a roaring success. In fact, we were going broke. Henrietta was about our only customer and our best advertisement. She may have looked like a little white-haired bird with toothpick legs, but after six months she could throw your dad over her shoulder with one hand." Dad nodded in agreement.

"But what about Jim Bob?" I asked.

"I'm getting to that," said Uncle Harley, not one to be rushed. "Pass the yogurt, please, Judith."

He dropped a huge dollop of yogurt on his brown rice. "One day a few weeks before you were born, a skinny little man in railroad stripe overalls appeared at the door. His hair was red as a stoplight, curled in tight ringlets all over his head."

"But what caught my attention were his eyes," said Mom. "They were bluer than a Kansas sky."

"You've never been to Kansas, Judith," scolded Uncle Harley, unhappy to have his story interrupted again.

"As I was saying, this skinny little fellow walked up to the desk and said, 'I need a new body!'

"'That's our specialty,' said your mother, pulling him in before he could change his mind.

"She did all the talking, while your father demonstrated. Then they showed him some 'before' and 'after' pictures and that did it. I handed him a six-month contract and he signed with a bony freckled hand, *Jim Bob Smiley*."

"He was anything but smiley," interjected Mom. "He looked so forlorn, even his freckles drooped. But he came faithfully every day. We kept him for dinner many times."

Desperate, I thought, or else very hungry.

Uncle Harley ignored Mom's interruption. "He had what it takes, Pitt, m' boy. He lifted and pushed and pulled and heaved and sweated without a complaint. And having to pass through the health-food store every day, he became acquainted with Henrietta. She soon had him gulping megavitamins, chewing bee pollen, and sprinkling wheat germ on everything from raw-milk-and-honey milk shakes to organically grown salads."

"Yuck! Why did he do that?"

"He had a good reason, Pitt," said Dad. "Go on, Uncle Harley."

Uncle Harley's eyebrows quivered. "I shall, if you all will listen." I slid down in my chair and nibbled my whole-wheat bread.

"Bit by bit," continued Uncle Harley, "between sets of push-ups and sit-ups, Jim Bob told me his whole sad story."

Chapter 4

"Born and raised in a snug little hollow called Hogsbreath, nestled in the Ozarks, Jim Bob published the town newspaper, the *Hogsbreath Herald*," Uncle Harley continued. "He also ran a neat pig farm he called J.B.'s Place. It kept him busy and happy, making bacon, curing ham, and frying chitlins. Happy, that is, until Charlotte came along.

"She arrived from Detroit with romantic notions of the Old South, looking for escape from city noise, filthy air, and congested streets. Tall, slim, and sophisticated, she was the most beautiful thing Jim Bob Smiley had ever seen. It didn't take him long to fall under her spell and pop the question. For a wedding present Jim Bob gave Charlotte a baby pig named Wilbur and renamed his farm 'Charlotte's Web,' after his favorite book.

"The honeymoon lasted until Charlotte realized that escape from city noise also meant escape from city entertainments, and that a pig farm, no matter how neat, still smelled like a pig farm."

I tried to imagine what a pig farm might smell like but finally decided it couldn't possibly smell any worse than the steamy green spinach loaf in front of me.

"Jim Bob tried his best to make Charlotte happy. But she was bored with Hogsbreath and unable to see the beauty of the forest." Uncle Harley leaned back in his chair and pulled thoughtfully on his watch chain. "She spent her nights complaining and her days safely immersed in the soaps. Finally, one day, she threw her clothes into a suitcase and went back to Detroit, leaving Jim Bob, Wilbur, and Charlotte's Web forever.

"At first Jim Bob simply didn't believe it. He was sure she would come back. When she didn't, Jim Bob stopped caring about anything. The *Hogsbreath Herald* disappeared from the Hogsbreath General Store. Jim Bob forgot to eat and he forgot to slop the pigs. He got thinner and the pigs got hungrier."

Uncle Harley chuckled. "Jim Bob found out just how hungry the pigs were when they tried to eat the banker who came to see why Jim Bob had stopped paying on his mortgage.

"Soon after, Jim Bob sold Charlotte's Web and all the pigs to pay the bank. With the money left over, he bought himself a trailer, loaded up his printing press, and headed west. He ended up right here in Desert Hills, where he opened up a print shop to put food on the table."

Uncle Harley shook his head. "But Jim Bob couldn't forget Charlotte. After six months, he boarded a bus for Detroit. Two days and fifteen minutes later he was pushing the doorbell of a small apartment in a shabby three-story building festooned with dozens of antennas of all sizes and shapes.

"Unfortunately for Jim Bob, Charlotte was at that very moment glued to her favorite soap, 'Generous Hospital.'

"Jim Bob's flushed face must have looked like one giant freckle," Uncle Harley mused. "'I c-came to t-take you home,' he said when she opened the door.

"Charlotte laughed. She aimed one long red fingernail at his striped overalls and said, 'Listen, you skinny runt. I need a real man! A real man like that!' She pointed at the television.

"On the small screen Jim Bob saw everything that he was not—a bronzed body builder rippling his muscles for a deodorant commercial. 'So come back when you look like that!' she said as she slammed the door.

"All the way back to the hotel, her words echoed in his brain, *skinny runt, skinny runt*. Yes, that's what he was."

I wriggled uncomfortably as Uncle Harley squinted his blue eyes at me. "Jim Bob vowed to change himself from a skinny runt to someone Charlotte couldn't resist. Then maybe, just maybe, he'd take her back."

Uncle Harley leaned back and breathed a satisfied sigh.

I waited for the next word. "Well?"

"Well, what?" asked Uncle Harley.

"Did he take her back? What happened after that? Did it work?"

"Those questions, m' boy," laughed Uncle Harley, "you will have to direct to Jim Bob himself."

Chapter 5

It took three more days of questions before I found out what Jim Bob had to do with our moving to Arizona. Tired of my pestering, Mom finally dragged out my baby book from under the box of old Christmas ornaments, blew off the dust, and filled in the details for me.

It seems I was born in the middle of the project to remake Jim Bob. My baby pictures show a chunky, sandy-haired kid with slightly crossed blue eyes and a thumb in his mouth. Under the pictures Mom had written, *Pitt (6 days). Look at those shoulders! . . . Pitt (3 months). Catch those muscles! . . . Pitt (6 months). Superchamp!*

They had plans for me. I was going to be the greatest athlete the world, or at least Detroit, had ever seen. One picture shows Dad holding me in his arms while he does flips on the trampoline. The next shows Dad wiping strained peas off his white T-shirt.

"Mom, why am I wearing a bib in all these pictures?" I asked.

Mom peered over my shoulder at the baby book. "Last measure of defense. You had a permanent trickle from your nose to your mouth and another drooly trickle from your mouth down your chin. You were so allergic, you couldn't eat and breathe at the same time, Pitt. That's why you always wore a bib stuffed with tissues.

"We knew we had to get you out of Detroit," Mom went on. "And it was Jim Bob who provided the chance."

Then she told me how Jim Bob's bankroll became weaker as his body became stronger, until one day he announced he was broke. Jim Bob, Mom and Dad, Uncle Harley, Henrietta, and a snotty-nosed toddler with a tissue-stuffed bib all sat down to discuss this predicament. For the truth was, we were broke, too.

"All I have," said Jim Bob, "is a two-bedroom trailer and a small print shop in Arizona."

"And all we have," said Mom, "is this gym, a child who's allergic to city air, and a lifetime supply of tissues and bibs."

Everyone looked at the floor. Then Henrietta came up with an idea. "Trade!"

"Trade?"

"Of course. Trade the gym for the trailer and the print shop in Arizona!"

They all began to smile and nod their heads. I kept drooling onto my bib. And that's how Mom, Dad, Uncle Harley, and I ended up in Heaven Hill Trailer Park in Desert Hills, Arizona, and Henrietta and Jim Bob became partners in the body-building business in Detroit.

Uncle Harley did so well with the print shop that we bought a bigger trailer for us, and Uncle Harley kept Jim Bob's for himself. Dad started teaching exercise classes, and Mom became manager of Heaven Hill Trailer Park and substitute teacher for girls' P.E. at Desert Hills High.

Chapter 6

The best thing about Heaven Hill, I'd recently decided, was catching the school bus on the corner. It used to be the worst thing, or at least the most boring, watching fifteen little kids shoving in line while ten more ran around in the street looking for Frank Schneider, "Mr. Cool," in his new Trans Am sports car. But one day toward the end of September that all changed.

Maybe it was how I woke up that gave me the feeling that something was going to happen. I was dreaming I was being tied with ropes that wound around my wrists and up my arms. I punched out at my attacker.

"Wake up, Pitt!" As I opened my eyes, Dad whipped the tape measure off and dangled it in front of my face. I couldn't focus on the number he was marking with his thumbnail. All I could see was the smile on his face. "Look at that! You've gained a half-inch on those biceps."

By then I was wide awake. "Pitt, you're lookin' good!" he proclaimed proudly, giving my stomach a jab.

A month ago I would have been gasping for air after one of Dad's playful jabs.

I took my morning run and tanked up on Mom's homemade granola, which made me late, since I had to blast the dried prunes out of my braces with the Water-Pik. When I got to the bus stop, Alex was already there.

"Take a look at that." He jerked his head toward the front of the line.

"Becky?"

"Look again, Pitt."

Becky was there, all right. But she wasn't alone. She was talking to someone with hair like honey, flowing halfway down her back. You could tell she was new to the Arizona desert, because her skin was as white as milk. She and Becky made quite a contrast, since Becky's as brown as a pecan and has her dark hair cut almost as short as mine.

"Do you think that's . . . ?"

"Let's find out." Alex and I edged into a group of little kids to get a better look.

"Alex, it's the French-vanilla girl!" She looked even better than that day in Sarah's.

Alex whistled under his breath. "I know . . . the black Mercedes girl."

My tongue ran a quick inspection of my braces for bits of dried prune. I shifted my five books and three notebooks to one arm and took a casual stance.

" . . . so Daddy and I had already moved in, but

Mother insisted I go back to Atlanta to keep her company until we sold the house," the girl was saying. "Now I have to start school at Desert Hills a whole month late!"

Alex and I moved a little closer.

"Ya can't have ups!" yelled the red-headed kid behind Becky.

"So, who wants 'em?" I smiled at him and grabbed the notebook that was slipping out from under my arm. "Watch it, brat!" I whispered. Becky threw us a glance over her shoulder.

"Pitt, did you finish your algebra?" Alex asked loudly.

"What algebra? We didn't have any algebra."

"Wise up!" he hissed under his breath.

"Oh, that algebra." The corner of my biology book landed like a sledge hammer on my left big toe. "Ow!" I grabbed my wounded foot and dropped the rest of my books on the sidewalk.

By the time I collected my stuff, Alex was looking the other way, pretending he didn't know me, Becky was bent over laughing, and the French-vanilla girl was grinning, showing a perfect row of white teeth that my orthodontist would've been proud of. For once I was glad to see Frank Schneider careen around the corner in his black Trans Am, scattering the kids in the street, who shrieked as they ran for the curb.

_____

During English class, Alex passed me a note.

Her name's Melissa Benson. She just moved here from Georgia and she lives about a block from Heaven Hill in that fancy brown house with the iron fence. Her dad is some kind of high-powered businessman from Atlanta.

"You're a pretty good detective," I congratulated him after class. "So, she's rich as well as beautiful. I don't stand a chance."

"Sure you do, Pitt. You haven't even tried. By the way, she plays flute, too."

I decided right there and then to pick up my trombone again and change from study hall back to band. Why not both sports and music? I reasoned. Maybe Melissa goes for musical muscle men.

Chapter 7

"Well, make up your mind, Pitt Kowalski!" grumbled Mr. Jordan when I walked in the next day carrying my schedule change and my trombone. But he smiled as he stroked his mustache and pointed with his baton at my old seat, still empty and waiting—last-chair trombone. I knew they couldn't replace me.

I sat down and put my slide together. "Hey, Lance." I poked the next-to-last-chair trombonist. "Got any new flutes in band lately?"

Lance opened his spit valve and gave my shoe a shower. "New flutes? Naw. Why?"

The door opened, and in walked Melissa, blinking her big blue eyes in sort of a lost way.

"Go-o-o-lly!" breathed Lance.

Mr. Jordan looked up suspiciously to see why the band was so quiet. When he spied Melissa with her flute case, he smiled. "A flautist! Just what we need!" He pulled a chair into the first row for her.

"I won't be in band all the time if I make cheerleader," warned Melissa cheerfully.

Mr. Jordan sighed and mumbled something to

the ceiling about the sacrifice of art to the perennial pursuit of popularity. Desert Hills was so small that in order to play a concert or field a team, the music and athletics departments had to share kids. No one hated that more than Mr. Jordan.

He clipped a stray hair from his mustache and laid his scissors on the podium. "As some of you know," he began, "this is my last year at Desert Hills High. After thirty years of lecturing, threatening, scolding, pushing, and pulling students toward a love of music and a reasonable knowledge of how to make it, I'm retiring."

Some of the girls started to sniffle. "Now I didn't tell you this to cause a scene," continued Mr. Jordan, "but to explain why I am so excited. Ever since I began directing I've had a dream, but I never thought it would come true until now." It was embarrassing to see a grown man get so emotional, especially Mr. Jordan, who had always been unflappable.

"The good news arrived just this week. I hope you will be as happy and excited about it as I am."

Not an eyelid blinked as he unfolded an official-looking letter, adjusted his bifocals, and began to read.

From the United States Independence Day Celebration Committee, Washington D.C., to Mr. Eugene Jordan, Band Director, Desert Hills High School, Desert Hills, Arizona.

Dear Mr. Jordan:

This is to inform you that the Desert Hills High School Band is hereby invited to represent the great state of Arizona in the Independence Day Parade to be held in Washington, D.C., July 4 of next year.

Plans are already underway for the best celebration ever, and we feel that the Desert Hills High School Band will make a valuable contribution to the festivities. You may also want to take advantage of your visit to see the sights of our nation's capital.

Please respond at your earliest convenience.
Sincerely,
John C. McGregor, Chairman

Everybody started talking at once. Mr. Jordan held up his hands. "Now for the bad news," he said. "I have done some research with Mr. Evans, your principal, and, the nearest we can figure, it will cost about $40,000 to get us to Washington and back."

"Oh," eighty-five voices moaned at the same time.

"Don't look so defeated," he added quickly. "We can probably get much of the money donated. And if you're willing to work, we can earn the rest."

Melissa waved her hand in the air. "Mr. Jordan, my daddy can help. He's raised money for lots of projects."

"Wonderful, Melissa! Perhaps he would coordinate our fund raising. You students can also come up with ideas of your own. So, what do you say? What will our answer to Mr. McGregor be?"

"Yes!!!"

Mr. Jordan looked up with an expression I'd never seen before. If he weren't so tough, I could swear I saw tears in his eyes.

All day I thought about the news. A band trip to Washington was the perfect send-off for Mr. Jordan's last year. And just imagine—3,000 miles with Melissa Benson! But $40,000 was a lot of money. I hoped Melissa's dad knew how to do it.

I tried to come up with a good money-making idea as I did my sit-ups after school. But all I could think of was long honey-blond hair and big blue eyes.

"Come to dinner!" Mom yelled. The kitchen smelled like spinach again. I was relieved when Dad appeared at the door waving an envelope in his hand.

"Letter from Henrietta!"

Even dinner waited for letters from Henrietta to be read aloud. I sank into the nearest chair to listen. Dad slit the envelope with a table knife, unfolded the letter, and began to read.

Dear Judith, Tom, Harley, and Pitt,
    I hope this letter finds you all well, exercising, and eating right. The HHFS (that's Henrietta's

Health Food Store) is doing a great business and I'm busier than ever.

I had a minor problem a couple of weeks ago, however. A young man decided to help himself to the contents of the cash register by behaving quite belligerently and waving a little black revolver in the air.

But the problem was rather quickly—and cleverly, I thought (but I'm not one to brag)—solved when I slammed the cash-register drawer on his fingers, kicked him in the shin, and threw him over my head into the shelf of blackstrap molasses. He hit that molasses like a duck in a mud puddle! Molasses and glass flew from one end of the store to the other!

Oh, there was quite a mess, believe me. He was scrambling to his feet when Jim Bob, hearing the commotion, came running down the stairs. A pool of molasses sent Jim Bob flying in the air and sliding across the floor on his bottom. He landed right on top of that unfortunate young man and sat there, glued, while I called the police.

But I'm forgetting the most exciting part of all! The WNRS News van arrived with the patrol car, filmed the arrest, and interviewed Jim Bob for the evening news. Since then, our business has picked up so much I have had to hire extra help.

That's why Jim Bob and I decided to invest in

a series of TV commercials, and now WNRS even wants him to do a daily exercise show!

I do believe Jim Bob is becoming a household word in this city. Even Charlotte, whom he has never gotten over, was impressed when she saw him on TV. She signed up for an exercise class and, boy, does she need it! Jim Bob hardly recognized her after all these years of TV dinners. But to him she's still beautiful. Love is blind, as they say.

Well, enough of this prattling on. Soak up some sunshine for us and let us know what's cooking on Heaven Hill.

Love,

Henrietta

"What's cooking" turned out to be exactly what I'd suspected. Dad finished reading the letter and headed for the stove.

"What have we here, Judith?" He lifted the lid from a pot, letting a cloud of greenish steam billow into the air.

"Don't open that!" Mom charged to the stove. Dad banged down the lid. "That's Soybeans and Spinach Deluxe."

At the table Mom heaped the green goo on to my pile of brown rice. "Like it, Pitt?" she asked as I twirled the long strands of spinach around my fork like spaghetti. "It's my invention."

I exhaled and stuffed my mouth with the drippy gob on my fork. "M-m-g-f-f-d!" I answered. I really didn't mind healthy food, but why did it have to taste so healthy?

"Don't talk with your mouth full, Pitt," said Dad. Somehow I managed to finish Mom's good-for-you food.

"May I be excused? I've got tons of homework." That line usually worked when there were dirty dishes around. "And I've got to practice my trombone."

Dad tried hard to work his mouth into a smile. "Do your trombone early, Pitt. We don't want the neighbors calling to complain."

"Okay, Dad."

A neighbor did call, but it was only Becky being a smart aleck. "Pitt, are you sick? There's all this moaning coming from your room."

"Very funny, Becky," I said. "I've just recovered, so you can hang up now." I put away my trombone and tackled three pages of algebra homework. Then I did a few more push-ups before I went to bed.

Chapter 8

When I got to the bus stop the next morning, little kids were all over the place, but Becky and Alex were nowhere to be seen. Melissa stood close to the street, all by herself. Perfect opportunity!

As I was trying to think of something to say, a black Trans Am squealed around the corner. Melissa jumped back from the curb. Schneider was, of course, trying to flatten everything between his house and the high school. Dumb clod, scaring Melissa. Before his rich grandfather gave him that car, he was just another pimply-faced passenger on Bus 44. Funny how a set of wheels can change a kid's personality.

"Hi!" The shout left my ears ringing.

"Oh, it's you, Becky."

"Want to meet her?"

"What? Meet who?" Sometimes it seemed like Becky could read my mind.

"Look, Marshmallow, I know you're dying to meet her." Becky pushed her glasses up on her nose.

"Becky, one person who called me that ended up with a bloody nose," I threatened.

Becky smiled. "I know, Pitt. That was five years

ago, when you were chasing me. You tripped over your skateboard, hit me in the face with your elbow, fell down, and broke your arm. Remember?"

Lucky for her, Alex showed up and pulled me to one side. "Just be ready," he whispered.

"Ready?" But he had already walked to where Melissa was standing, set down his books, and started talking history with her. It sure looked easy enough. "Hey, Pitt!" he called. My knees turned to Jell-O.

"Here's your big chance," Becky whispered through her grin as she followed me.

"Melissa, this is Pitt," said Alex. I was thankful he didn't lay my whole name on her at once.

"Ooh, I just love unusual names!" Her eyes were so big and blue I could have drowned in them. "Where ever did you get a name like Pitt?"

"I was porn in Bittspurgh .... I mean, born in Pittsburgh." Heat waves swelled up my neck and flooded into my face. Niagara Falls poured from my armpits.

"See, my mom was running in the Pittsburgh Marathon when she went into labor. She ran right into Pittsburgh Memorial Hospital. I got a special award for being the youngest participant .... That's why they named me Pitt."

Melissa looked at Alex and Becky. "Is he for real?"

"He's not putting you on," said Alex, pounding my back to prove I was real. "His mom and dad have trophies for running and weight lifting, and his uncle played for the Detroit Lions."

Melissa sighed. "Ooh, I just *lo-o-o-ove* athletes. Don't you, Becky?"

Becky opened her mouth, then closed it again. A strangled sound came out of her throat before she answered. "Sure, Melissa." I could have kicked her.

At lunchtime Alex caught up with me at the lockers. "You made quite an impression," he said as we put our books away. "In history Melissa asked me what your last name was." I ducked as he slammed his locker door closed. I hated having a bottom locker.

"And how long did it take her to stop laughing?"

"Pitt, loosen up. I think she likes you. Just be yourself." Linda Simmons ran up from behind and grabbed him around the waist.

"Hi, honey." She leaned over his shoulder and gave him a kiss on the cheek.

"I'd rather be you," I replied, watching them go off hand in hand toward the cafeteria. "Pitt, m' boy— as Uncle Harley would say—you've got a long way to go." I slammed my locker shut and shook the cramps out of my legs as I straightened up.

After school Becky came to shoot baskets.

"Are you kidding? Football tryouts tomorrow."

"Sure, Marsh. *Ooh*, I just *lo-o-o-o-ove* athletes!" Becky pushed up her glasses and walked off.

"Jealous!" I shouted.

It would have been more fun to shoot baskets, even with Becky, but I had this vision of racing down the football field to the roar of the crowd. I imagined Melissa in the end zone, arms wide, honey hair blowing in the wind.

I went inside and started my exercises before Uncle Harley could come to badger me. Two hundred sit-ups and one hundred push-ups—that's where I was. I could hold Dad off for three minutes now before he whipped me in arm wrestling.

The next morning I mixed up a breakfast shake of milk, egg, banana, pineapple, honey, and vanilla. It was my invention. I called it Fastbreak, because I drank it fast and made a break for the door before Mom could make me eat her double-fortified bran biscuits and scrambled tofu. Someday, I decided, I was going to write my own recipe book for healthy food.

Melissa and Becky were waiting at the bus stop. "Hey, Pitt!" called Melissa.

She was wearing a mint green halter dress, and I tried not to stare at her creamy shoulders as she gave me a big smile. I smiled back just the way I'd practiced in the mirror—a real dazzler.

"You have granola in your braces," Becky said. I clamped my mouth shut. Then I remembered I hadn't eaten granola.

"Well, at least I don't have oatmeal in my hair . . . or maybe a bird just flew over." Becky made a face, but she couldn't help feeling her hair, just to make sure. I knew her mother made her eat oatmeal every morning.

"You two are really good friends, aren't you?" Melissa laughed. She laid her hand lightly on my arm, and a tingle raced all the way down to my feet. I even smiled at the roaring black streak that was Frank Schneider on his way to school.

The memory of that tingle carried me through four pages of algebra problems, a history test, and football tryouts. I made third-string left guard—better than I expected. Alex got starting quarterback, of course. Coach Fernandez told us to swim laps or jog every day.

Jog? I could fly! My Nikes hardly touched the ground all the way home.

Chapter 9

The weekend at last! No six o'clock alarm, no two-and-a-half-minute shower, no race to the bus stop. Laps in Alex's pool instead of a sweaty two-mile jog with Dad, then perhaps a slow bike ride to Sarah's Ice Cream Parlor via the brown house with the iron fence.

But there was no escaping Mom's gigantic extra-healthy breakfast on Saturdays. Dad was already digging into a whole-wheat-bran waffle, and a tower of them was about to topple off my plate.

"Mom, how can I swim laps if I eat all that?"

"It'll build your strength for next Saturday's game. Eat," she ordered.

I counted the waffles in the stack. "It'll build a belly, that's all." A familiar double knock on the back door told me I was saved from that towering mountain of healthfulness.

"Good morning, all! Um-m-m, Judith, what a smell!"

"Hi, Uncle Harley," Mom said. "Sit down and help Pitt eat those waffles. He thinks they'll make him fat."

Uncle Harley didn't need a second invitation.

While he piled his plate, I found a couple of soft pears in the refrigerator, a plastic bag half full of chopped pecans, and another of shredded coconut.

"I'll make my own, Mom." I sliced the pears into a pan and put them on the stove with a few drops of water and some honey. The sweet fruity smell filled the kitchen. I poured the waffle batter into the waffle iron and sprinkled it with pecans and coconut. When I finally poured the honey-pear syrup on my waffle, Dad stopped chewing.

"Hey, Pitt, that looks good!"

Mom joined in. "Smells heavenly!"

Uncle Harley licked his lips. "Sure would like to taste your concoction, Pitt, m' boy."

So I had to cook five more waffles and write the recipe for Mom before I could get off to Alex's. With a little imagination, even healthy food could taste great, I decided.

I felt so good that I left my bike home and ran the three blocks to Alex's house. Along the way I passed Becky, wired for sound, speed, and accuracy.

She was running flat out, with a pedometer on her shoe, a cassette player on her belt, and earphones on her head. I knew from the look of concentration in her eyes that she was listening to a training tape.

She had broken two track records last year and was determined to break another one at the All-Region Track Meet in June. No wonder my parents treated her like a member of the Kowalski family!

Between the slats of the wooden gate, I could see

Alex skimming leaves off the pool with the long-handled skimmer. His backyard was enclosed by six-foot stucco walls. The big kidney-shaped pool took up most of the area, and a flagstone patio wound around a dozen lemon and grapefruit trees. An old Ping-Pong table sat on one side and lawn chairs on the other. It looked cool and inviting after my run.

Alex banged the skimmer on the trash can to empty it. "Hi, Pitt. Jump in!" he called as I opened the gate.

I stripped off my T-shirt and looked down at my jeans. "Wouldn't you know it. I forgot my trunks."

"Never mind. You can wear a pair of mine."

In his bedroom, Alex dug around in a drawer and threw me a red-and-blue-striped racing suit. That is, it used to be a racing suit, but it looked like it came in last place.

"What happened to this?" I held up the limp piece of nylon.

"Oh," said Alex, "That must be the suit my cousin Carlos borrowed last summer. He's a little heavy."

"Heavy! He must do sumo wrestling on the side."

Alex sighed. "Put it on, Pitt. We're gonna swim laps, not model swimsuits."

As he admired his bronzed muscles in the mirror, I pulled on the suit and grumbled under my breath. By bulging my stomach out, I could make it stay up when I walked, but it sagged in front and bagged behind. At any rate, it was better than a six-block run to my house and back.

Alex grabbed two towels from the bathroom and pitched them at me on the way out. I watched as he flipped off the board and hit the water with barely a ripple. The late-morning sun beat warm on my shoulders, a perfect day for swimming.

I climbed on the board and bounced a couple of times, holding on to the saggy, baggy suit with one hand. Voices sounded from the street. I bounced a few more times, bracing myself for the cold shock of the water. Then I heard the squeal of bike brakes in the driveway. One of the voices definitely belonged to Linda Simmons. The other one sounded like Melissa.

"Alex," I hissed down at him, "you didn't tell me girls were coming!"

Alex scowled. "Nobody told me either."

I dove off quickly, straight to the bottom. But I had forgotten about cousin Carlos and the swimsuit. As soon as I hit the water, the suit took off in the opposite direction. I made a grab for it as it brushed past my ankles. But it escaped my fingers, floated to the top, and hung there like a red-and-blue jellyfish. There was nothing to do but swim after it.

"Help!" I whispered to Alex, who was halfway up the ladder. The girls were rattling the gate.

"Alex? Alex, it's Linda."

They pushed the gate open. I grabbed the suit and

jammed one foot into it. Alex had swum back and was treading water in front of me, splashing around to make a screen. He was laughing so hard I thought he might drown. I wouldn't have cared right then, especially if cousin Carlos had joined him.

Linda gave us a puzzled look before she stripped off her cover-up and pulled out a mirror to check her make-up and pat her golden hair into place.

"I brought Melissa over for a swim." As if we couldn't see Melissa standing there, looking as good as whipped cream in her raspberry jumpsuit.

Alex was laughing too hard to talk. I was trying to get the other foot in the suit, stay behind Alex, and smile at Melissa all at once. Then I discovered I had it on upside down, with both feet in the same leg hole.

"What's the joke?" asked Linda. Alex was still bobbing up and down in the water. "What's the matter with Pitt?"

I sank under the water, vowing to come up with the suit on or not come up at all. Two splashes told me the girls were in the pool. Finally, I emerged, half-drowned but decently covered.

Still laughing, Alex swam to the end of the pool and kicked off on his first lap. It was Linda's turn to scowl as she watched him stroke smoothly past us.

"Guess what, Pitt. I made cheerleader first try!" announced Melissa.

"Just like I did last year," added Linda loudly, looking at Alex.

My vision flashed in front of my eyes like a fifteen-second commercial—the roar of the crowd, the pounding of feet behind me, Melissa, arms wide . . .

"Pitt? Pitt, what's the matter?" asked Melissa. "You look funny."

"What? Oh, nothing. Just thinking of something."

"Well, aren't you going to congratulate me?"

"Yeah, sure. I mean, that's great, Melissa! But . . . are you still in band? You aren't going to miss the trip to Washington, are you?"

"Mr. Jordan said I could be in both. He needs flutes. I think he needs Daddy, too." Melissa smiled. "Did you know Daddy is handling the fund raising? His company, I mean, Benson and Associates. Forty thousand dollars is nothing to them."

Alex doused us with water as he flipped on his back and kicked past. Linda glared at his wake and checked her hair to see how much damage he had done.

"Let's get out of the pool and sit on the patio." Her suggestion sounded more like a command.

"Uh, no . . . I think I'll stay here."

"But why, Pitt? You're not even swimming," she insisted. I tried one of Alex's noncommittal smiles, and got a disgusted look in return.

"Got anything to drink?" Melissa called to Alex. "I'm getting out. Come on, Pitt."

"Uh, no . . . I like the water."

The three of them drank lemonade on the patio

47

while I floated in the pool, gripping my suit, thinking of what I would like to do to Alex and cousin Carlos, and watching my body slowly pucker into a pale prune. "Guess we'd better go," Linda announced to Melissa at last. She waited for Alex to protest.

He just smiled. "Then Pitt and I will finish our laps."

As Melissa opened the gate she called, "Pitt, are you going to play football or trombone at the game next Saturday?"

I laughed. "I think Mr. Jordan's glad I made the football team. He hasn't chopped his mustache once since I told him." I paddled in circles to stop my teeth from chattering. "I'm playing left guard." I didn't tell her third string.

She smiled deliciously. "Maybe I'll see you at the dance afterward."

Oh, if I only knew how to dance!

Chapter 10

The next week we band members visited every business in Desert Hills. Mr. Benson, Melissa's father, ordered pizzas and chocolate bars for us to sell, and we advertised on the radio for our weekly car washes.

Football dissolved into a blur of practice and exercise, exercise and practice.

"Hit 'em harder! Harder!"

"Block 'em! Block 'em!"

"Tackle him! . . . Not *him*, the one with the ball!"

Saturday night came much too soon. The locker room smelled of sweat, athlete's foot powder, and excitement. Everybody talked at once and nobody listened.

"Man, you look massive!" said Alex as I slipped a gold jersey over my head.

"Yeah," I agreed. "Now if I could just wear these shoulder pads to school!" I felt like a Roman gladiator. "Ol' number 13 is going to knock them down like bowling pins."

Coach Fernandez snorted. "Ol' number 13 had

better put his shirt on right side out. You're number 31, Kowalski!"

He slapped me on the rear. "Okay, guys, let's go out and show Northside how football should be played!"

The crowd cheered, and the band struck up the "Desert Hills Fight Song" as we jogged single file out of the locker room, through the gate, and down the field.

I spotted Mom and Dad and Uncle Harley as I passed the stands. And there was Melissa with the other cheerleaders. Wow! She was looking right at me.

Is she waving at me, I wondered. She *is* waving at me!

"Oof!" A helmet slammed into my back. I landed in a heap. "Bam!" Cleats ground a tattoo into my calf.

"Kowalski!" roared Coach Fernandez in my ear. "Who told you to stop in the middle of the field?"

"Sorry, Coach." I felt like disappearing. Tank Billings, our 210-pound center, pulled me up and pushed me in the direction of our bench.

That's where I stayed. Alex got away from Northside's tacklers and ran thirty yards for a touchdown in the first quarter. The score stood 7–0 at the half, and I hadn't moved. Melissa kept looking at the bench. Was she wondering why I wasn't playing? . . . Or was she looking over the other guys?

After halftime I made it from the locker room to

the bench without a hitch. Northside scored two quick touchdowns, and I could hear Uncle Harley yelling advice to the coach. Was he really shouting, "Put in Kowalski"?

We were down 10 to 12 with only three minutes to go. Coach was pacing up and down.

"Kowalski! Get in there!"

All of a sudden I was sweating. Why did Richard Norris sprain his ankle? Why did Andy Minola hurt his knee? Why did I go out for football?

Before I knew it, I was running out on the field. One part of me was thinking, Pitt, you're nothing but crazy. No girl's worth getting bashed in for. Another part was saying, Go! Now's your chance!

I took my place in the line, noting that the guy in the red-and-white jersey facing me looked a lot like a bulldog with acne. He was growling and showing big pointed teeth. I smiled, friendly-like. I wanted to explain to him that it was only a game after all.

The center snapped the ball. I lunged forward and found out the bulldog was really a brick wall. He spun me around three times before I fell. The sky filled with rainbows of red and white, then purple and gold. Through the maze of legs, I could see Tank Billings three yards behind the line of scrimmage, sitting like king of the mountain on top of their ball carrier.

"Come on!" called Alex. "It's third and nineteen. They've got to pass this time. Sack 'em!"

I felt less like a gladiator and more like one of the Christians about to face the lions. My counterpart wasn't growling this time. He was grinning.

I bared my teeth and let out a menacing snarl from deep in my throat. The ball was snapped.

Two hairy arms tried to fold me in half. I held my ground. Round and round we went, like two dancers who both want to lead. The field lights spun faster and faster. They reminded me of the sparklers Dad used to buy me at Halloween. Then the sparklers disappeared and the ground came up and socked me.

I scrambled to my feet. The field lights were still on their merry-go-round. Where was the ball?

Screams poured from the stands. "Get 'em! Get 'em!" Their quarterback faded to pass. Three of our guys reached him at the same time. Desperately, he flicked the ball over their heads. It sailed like an arrow . . . right toward me!

The ball hit me hard in the stomach. I couldn't believe my luck. Covering it with both arms, I made for a huge hole in the defense. The Northside players were sure caught off guard.

I took off like the wind. The crowd was roaring. Cheering, yelling, screaming exploded in my ears, driving me on.

I flew down the field, wind blowing cold on my face, feet pounding behind me. My dream was coming true!

Behind the goal posts our cheerleaders were

pointing and waving and jumping up and down. They were shouting something that I couldn't make out. Where was Melissa? The goal line was thirty yards away. . . . Feet thudded behind me. There she was. . . . Why was she covering her face? . . . Only twenty-five yards! Feet pounded beside mine.

A familiar face came abreast. "Quick! Give me the ball, Pitt!"

"Alex! Why?" He had a panicked look in his eyes. I couldn't believe my best friend wanted to steal my glory. I hugged the ball and kept running.

Another face, this one a lot bigger, loomed on the other side. "Don't be an idiot, Pitt! Hand off the ball to Alex!" Was this a conspiracy?

I had no chance to think about it as Tank Billings bumped me hard, and Alex grabbed the ball from my arms.

As I tumbled to the turf, flattened by 210 pounds of purple and gold, the roar of the crowd became deafening.

"Why?" I gasped as I sat up.

"Look!" said Tank, pointing downfield. Alex was zigzagging his way through a pack of red-and-white jerseys toward the goal line—the other goal line.

Tank wiped his hands on his pants and pulled me to my feet. "Pitt, you were running the wrong way."

Chapter 11

Sunday morning I had already decided to stay in bed for the rest of my life when Alex called.

"Hey, man, it could happen to anybody."

"Yeah," I replied. "But it didn't happen to me; I happened to it. So how does it feel to be carried off the field on the team's shoulders? . . . And how was the dance?"

He ignored my first question. "Hey, the dance was great. Melissa was looking for you. You should've come. I told her we planned the whole play to put Northside off guard."

"I hope you didn't expect her to believe you. Who did she dance with?"

"A lot of guys . . . Tank Billings, Frank Schneider . . . I don't know. You weren't there, Pitt. So she couldn't dance with you."

"You're right. Her feet are probably better off, too. I'm glad she had a good time. Good night, Alex." I hung up the phone and buried myself in bed again.

Breakfast sounds were coming from the kitchen. "Wh-r-r-r." Mom was juicing oranges. "Clank!" She put the skillet on the stove. My stomach rumbled. On second thought, I decided, as I threw on a shirt and jeans, I'll eat, then go back to bed for the rest of my life.

"Pitt! Pitt, come quick!"

Something must have caught fire. I raced down the hall. "I'm coming!" My heart was pounding as I burst into the kitchen.

"Look!" Mom squealed, pointing at the television. A well-muscled fellow in a blue stretch jumpsuit was demonstrating controlled knee bends as he carried on a lively one-way conversation with the camera in an easy going Southern drawl. I knew that boyish freckled face and curly red hair.

"Jim Bob!"

Mom grinned. "Yes, it's Jim Bob. He's been syndicated. He'll be seen all over the USA!"

Dad, still panting from his morning run, pushed open the screen door. "He made it! The boy made it!" he exclaimed. He sounded proud, as if Jim Bob were his own son.

While Mom phoned Uncle Harley with the news, I took over the tofu that she had crumbled into the skillet. I added chopped green onions and peppers to it, sprinkled garlic powder on top, and squirted a dash of Tabasco. Now it smelled like something to look forward to. I poured the beaten eggs on top and added some chopped tomato and grated cheddar cheese over the whole thing.

"My son, the chef," Mom said, hanging up the phone.

"Yes," I agreed. "And the world-famous left guard."

"Now, Pitt . . . " There was a knock at the door.

"Becky! Come on in," said Dad. I had forgotten we were supposed to study biology. Of all the kids in class, I had to end up with Becky Rivera for a lab partner.

In her blue-and-gold sweat suit, Becky looked like she had just walked out of a sports magazine. But something was wrong. Tears were streaming down her face.

"Hi, Mr. and Mrs. Kowalski. Hi, Pitt. I didn't mean to walk in on your breakfast."

"Gee, Becky, we don't mind," I told her. "You don't need to cry about it." Mom patted her on the back.

"No, no," Becky protested. "I'm not crying. That is, I'm crying, but not because anything's wrong. I'm crying because of these." She pointed at her eyes.

"There's nothing wrong with brown eyes," I assured her in my big-brother voice. "Some of my best friends have brown eyes."

"Oh, Pitt, don't be silly." She stood on tiptoe and stuck her face in mine. "I'm talking about my new contact lenses. They're making my eyes water."

"Oh." I hadn't even noticed she wasn't wearing her glasses. "Well, sit down and have some vitamin C. Vitamin C is good for everything."

Mom didn't know I was kidding. She set a glass of orange juice and two vitamin C tablets in front of Becky. Then she set her a place, so she had to stay for my Tofu Spanish Omelette.

Halfway through breakfast, Mom jumped up. I was afraid I had put in too much Tabasco. "See? See, Pitt? The vitamin C worked! Becky isn't crying anymore."

"How do you know it's the vitamin C?" I asked reasonably. "It might be the tofu, or the cheese, or the onions, or the garlic powder, or . . ." At that moment a size-11 running shoe made direct contact with my shin under the table. "But I'm sure you're right, Mom. Vitamin C is fantastic." Dad smiled approvingly from across the table.

"Well, would you look at that!" Becky exclaimed. "That's why my eyes felt so much better." She scooted two slivers of plastic off her plate and onto her napkin. "My contacts came right out, and I didn't even know it!"

Becky washed her contacts and put them back in their case. "It may take a while to get used to these." She finished off a second helping of omelette. "Hey, Pitt, I missed the game yesterday. How was it? Did we win?"

I laughed and told her how I ran the wrong way. I mean, she was going to hear about it sooner or later. And I told her about how Alex ran the ball back thirty-five yards, close enough for Jeff Lancaster to kick a field goal.

"So we won, 13–12! What did Coach Fernandez say when it was over?" she asked.

"Nothing. After the game he shook his head, put his hat on backward, and walked out of the locker room."

It was funny. I wasn't even embarrassed telling Becky about it. If she laughed at me, I'd laugh back at her. But what would the kids at school say? And what would Melissa say? Would she even talk to me at all? I tried not to think about it.

Chapter 12

When Monday morning rolled around, I considered being sick, but I knew I'd have to face school—and Melissa—sooner or later. I decided later was better, so I walked the three miles to school.

I started out at a brisk pace, but my trombone grew heavier with each step. Just as I was asking myself why I didn't play piccolo instead, the ground began to tremble under my feet. I turned around to check out the roar of a fast-approaching motor and walked right off the sidewalk into a pile of dog mess in Mrs. Frankenweiler's yard. A screech of rubber on asphalt followed, and Frank Schneider's black Trans Am flashed by. I caught a glimpse of blond hair blowing free in the wind on the passenger side.

Well, give me a new sports car and I'd have blond hair blowing from it, too. I scraped my left tennis shoe off on the grass, wondering if Mrs. Frankenweiler had traded in her Pekingese for a Great Dane. The exhaust fumes from the car, mingled with the odor from my shoe, took all the pleasure out of breathing. Finally I gave up on the shoe and started off for school again, trying to ignore the pungent smell that wafted up with each step.

The high school loomed ahead, windows winking in the morning sun. As I entered the front door, the warning bell sent everyone rushing to class, except for Alex, of course, who was never in a hurry, since he had algebra first period.

"Hey, Pitt, miss the bus?" He clapped me on the shoulder, then backed off. "What's that smell?"

"It's a long, messy story," I replied. Gratefully I set my trombone case down and squeezed in front of Alex's knees to open my locker. The odor coming from my shoe threatened to knock me out. I held my breath and twirled my combination lock quickly to the right, then left, then right again. "Move your feet, Alex. I can't even see my lock."

"Melissa must have missed it, too."

Why wasn't it opening? I twisted the dial again, and it finally came open. "What?"

"She wasn't on the bus, either. Hey, here she comes now."

Melissa hurried up the hall with somebody who looked only too familiar. The only difference was that now his slicked-back hair and Don Johnson chin were not framed by a Trans Am window. Exit time for me. I jerked out my English book, which triggered an avalanche. Quickly I stuffed everything back inside—four books, three notebooks, two slightly soft Milky Ways, a band sweater, five pencils, and last year's February issue of *Sports Illustrated*. I slammed the door and stood up.

Unfortunately, I had forgotten to make sure that Alex had closed his locker. *Twang-g-g-g-g!* Cymbals crashed together inside my head. Fog closed in. I smiled at Melissa and Frank Schneider like it was nothing. In the middle of the smile I heard a snicker, but I couldn't focus on where it came from. The hall went black except for the most marvelous multicolored glitter floating in front of my eyes. My knees buckled, and the world vanished.

Next thing I knew, I woke up in the sickroom. Nurse Leflar wiped my face with an icy washcloth and patted my hand.

"You poor, poor boy," she crooned happily. She loved company.

"I'm okay . . . except for my head . . . . Ouch!" I shouldn't have touched it. Nurse Leflar giggled and patted my hand again. My left foot felt strangely cold. Maybe I was paralyzed! Then I saw my left shoe on the edge of the sink, washed spotless.

"Thanks." I nodded painfully at the shoe.

"My pleasure!" she answered merrily. "You've had a rough morning from end to end!" She laughed at her clever joke.

Chapter 13

Mom was in the kitchen cooking, with her Sony Walkman earphones plugged in. Dad was outside jogging with Alex, who was thinking about track season already, just like Becky. It was Dad's third time out that day. He always found an excuse to leave when I played my trombone.

But I had to practice for the homecoming parade. I could have ridden on the float with the football team instead of marching with the band, but I figured Mr. Jordan needed me. Besides, trombones made up the first row, right behind the cheerleaders. At least this way I could be near Melissa.

She hadn't talked to me since that first football game. It was hard to believe she was really going out with that creep Schneider. Even a third-string left guard was more of an athlete than he was, I thought, as I marched to the kitchen.

"Left, right. Left, right. Horns up. Play!" I did fine just playing or just marching. It was when we had to do both at the same time that I panicked.

"Let's eat!" Mom called. "We're having yummy Soy-Nut Burgers with horseradish sauce!"

I put my trombone away and headed for the back door. "Oh . . . Mom, I just remembered. I have to help Alex with his math. I'll eat later." I was out and on my bike before she could say a word.

Phew! Close escape. Something definitely had to be done before I starved to death, I thought, as I biked to Alex's house.

A spicy chili-and-onion sizzle greeted me at the door. Alex's dad, in a business suit with a towel around his middle, hovered over a frying pan. "Hey, Pitt, come on in!" He hollered. "You're just in time for tacos."

Now that was real eating. Alex was happy to have help with his homework, and the tacos were more than enough reward.

After dinner we stretched out on Alex's bedroom floor, with wall-to-wall paper, pencils, algebra books, and two big bowls of my latest dessert invention: Banana Brainstorm.

I rolled over and patted my tight belly. "If I lived with you, I'd weigh as much as Melinda Potts," I sighed. "I love your dad's tacos."

Alex punched my stomach. "Even after six of them, you're still looking good, Pitt. I can't call you Marshmallow anymore."

I winced happily. "It's all those sit-ups I do every day. Come on, let's get to work."

Alex groaned. "But, Pitt, I still don't understand how you got that last answer." He stuffed another spoonful of strawberry yogurt and bananas in his mouth.

"Algebra's not that hard. It's not nearly as hard as making a first down when eleven guys are out to clobber you."

"Yeah, that's what my father says," Alex answered dejectedly. "But, for me, algebra's a lot harder. My dad can't understand that. I wish I were more like you, Pitt."

I dropped my pencil and stared at him. "You've got to be kidding, Alex. You've got everything going for you. I mean, you're good at every sport, and you've got Linda. . . . "

Alex laughed. "Or she's got me. Sometimes I wonder. Anyway, you can't be a jock all your life. Why are some subjects hard for me? My dad is so smart."

"And why do I trip over my feet? Look at my parents. Maybe we got switched as babies," I suggested. "Did your parents ever visit Pittsburgh?"

"No, my mom wasn't into running marathons when she was pregnant." The phone by his bed rang, and Alex let out a big sigh. "Hey, Pitt, do me a favor. Answer that, okay?"

"Sure, Alex." I picked up the receiver. "Hello?"

"Hello. Alex?"

"No, it's me, Pitt."

"Oh...Hi, Pitt. This is Linda. Is Alex there? I don't need to talk to him. I just need to know if he's there."

"Yeah, he's here. What do you want me to tell him?"

"Nothing. I'll see him tomorrow. Thanks, Pitt. Bye."

I hung up the phone. "That call was sorta for you." Alex stared out the window. He wrinkled his nose.

"Let's see. Give me three guesses. Linda, Linda, or Linda."

"Yeah. Hey, does she always check up on you like that?"

"It's getting worse," he answered. "I feel like I'm married already."

As I rode home, I could still taste those delicious tacos.

"Cumin and fresh cilantro, that's the trick," Alex's dad had explained. Why, even spinach and soybeans might not be bad wrapped in a warm tortilla.

I sat down and wrote all my food ideas on recipe cards before I went to bed. Somehow I was going to figure out a way to jazz up the menu in the Kowalski household.

Chapter 14

"Come on, Pitt!" Dad called. "I'll drop you at school if you'll hurry."

I bared my teeth in the mirror. No granola in the braces. As I straightened the gold tassels on my shoulders, I noticed my band pants were a little bit "high-water." Lucky I had long purple socks to match the grape-jelly uniform.

The soccer field outside the band room was jammed with horses and riders, bicycles, floats on flatbed trailers, shiny sports cars and old jalopies, football players, band members, cheerleaders in short jumpers and Homecoming Maids in long formals.

Mr. Evans, the principal, was giving out numbers and instructions. "Cheerleaders come first!" he shouted.

"Yay!" yelled the cheerleaders.

"Then the band."

"Yay!" we yelled more loudly.

"After that, go by your numbers. . . . Oh, and horses last!"

"Yay!" I shouted again, remembering Mrs. Frank-enweiler.

Mr. Jordan blew his whistle for quiet. "Band, line up!" He waved his mustache scissors in the air. "Cheerleaders, in front!"

Melissa turned around and smiled. Maybe my luck was changing at last. She looked terrific in her gold jumper and purple satin blouse. Her honey-colored hair was woven into one thick braid, tied with shiny purple and gold ribbons.

Mr. Jordan slipped his scissors into his pocket and clapped his hands. My eyes locked on Melissa's perfect braid dancing on her back as she warmed up.

"Pitt?" She blinked her blue eyes at me. "Would you tell Alex to call me? I need help with my history assignment."

"What? Oh, sure, Melissa." She talked to me!

Mr. Jordan blew his whistle, three short blasts. The snare drums began their *rat-a-tat-tat*, and the parade began.

Scattered applause and excited voices greeted us as we started up Coronado Street, flags waving proudly from the standards, cheerleaders high-stepping, hands on hips, short skirts swaying. The band followed with precision steps, trombones in the lead.

Four short whistle blasts, instruments up, snares tattooing the rhythm, and we burst into "Desert Hills Forever."

This was fun. It was even easy. The music made

me keep in step. In fact, I was playing and marching automatically. I looked at my shiny black loafers in amazement. The crowd clapped and cheered as we marched by. My trombone . . . my trombone. . . . What was the matter with my trombone?

"Ow! Ow! Pitt, what are you doing?"

It couldn't be . . . but it was. My trombone slide was somehow caught in Melissa's braid! There was nothing to do but keep on marching and try to wiggle it out.

"Pitt Kowalski, get that thing out of there! Ow!"

If only she wouldn't jerk her head. "Ouch! Pitt Kowalski, I'll get you for this."

What could I do? The ribbons were tangled around the spit valve release. I took two giant strides and got up close to her. With the trombone in one hand, I tried to untangle it while I marched.

"Ouch! You stepped on my heel!"

I prayed Mr. Jordan was on the other side of the band. Lance was laughing too hard to play. Little kids on the curb pointed and jumped up and down. "Look at that guy! What's he doing?"

I could hear the trumpets behind me dropping out of the music, one by one. Their notes were replaced by hoots of laughter. I jerked the ribbon. Melissa yelped. No use.

Out of nowhere Mr. Jordan appeared. His mustache wiggled up and down furiously. He looked at my trombone and Melissa's hair. Then, without a word, he whipped out his little scissors and snipped off the ribbons. Melissa sighed gratefully. I fell back into line and played the rest of the parade with purple and gold ribbons dangling from my trombone slide.

Chapter 15

"Melissa isn't talking to me again."

I closed my locker and stood up very carefully, keeping one eye on Alex's locker door. "What's the use of spending half my life pumping iron if she doesn't appreciate the fact that my chest is now thirty-seven and a half inches?"

Alex laughed. "Is that why you've been wearing those tight T-shirts lately? Just be cool and casual, man." He motioned with his head toward Melissa and Becky, who were hurrying in our direction. "Remember, cool and casual," he said over his shoulder as he left to meet Linda for lunch.

Okay. Cool and casual—that's what I'd be. Coolly, I leaned against the lockers. Casually flexing my biceps, I held up my algebra book and studied the table of contents. I took a deep breath and expanded my chest to its full thirty-seven and a half inches. I hoped Melissa would be suitably impressed by my pectorals and go right on, so I could exhale.

I should have known better.

"Hi, Pitt," Becky said with a silly grin. "Want to come eat with us?"

I shook my head and tried to smile. The veins in my forehead began to strain like ropes holding down a hot-air balloon. I shook my head again. I could feel my eyes bug out and my ears expand right along with my chest.

Melissa pulled Becky's sleeve. "Come on, Becky. I'm hungry."

Yes, go on, Becky, I prayed. I didn't want Melissa to see my chest cave in like a Florida sinkhole. They walked off, and I made myself count to five before exhaling, just to make sure they didn't hear the explosion. "One, two, three . . . "

Two strong brown arms flew around my waist. A small fist dug into my middle. "WHOOSH!" It felt like everything north of my toes left through my mouth.

I fell to my knees, coughing. "Becky! Why did you do that?"

"Pitt, thank God you're all right! Your face was turning blue! Lucky for you I learned the Heimlich manuever in health class."

I got to my feet. "Yeah, Becky. Lucky for me." I passed up lunch and collapsed in the library until it was time to go to band.

Mr. Jordan didn't mention the parade at all. He was too busy helping Mr. Benson pass out potato-supper tickets for us to sell.

Lance groaned. "Mr. Jordan, I've rung so many doorbells so many times, I've become a magician."

"A magician, Lance?" asked Mr. Jordan.

"Yeah. I can make curtains close and lights go out just by walking up somebody's front walk!"

Everybody laughed.

"I know what you mean," I said. "It happened to me at my own house last night."

That got a bigger laugh. "Okay, okay, wise guys." Mr. Jordan smiled as he tapped on a music stand with his baton.

But Mr. Benson was not amused. He cleared his throat and climbed on the podium. He was short and stout and had jowls that hung down like a bulldog's. It was hard to believe he was Melissa's father.

"Ladies and gentlemen," he growled, "if you intend on making this trip to Washington, you must be serious and businesslike. No one is going to drop the money in your laps." He looked meaningfully at the trombone section. Lance and I slid down in our chairs.

"Yeesh!" whispered Lance. "I'd hate to have a dad like that. Can't even take a joke."

Mr. Jordan tried not to smile. "Yes, boys and girls, Mr. Benson is right. It is terribly important to try our hardest. And the potato supper is going to be a terrific fund raiser. It will be our last one before Christmas. We expect to serve at least 500 people, and we already have an enthusiastic parent to supervise—Mrs. Kowalski. She assures me it will be an unforgettable experience."

I slid even lower in my chair. *My* mother? *My* mother was going to be in charge of serving 500 people? Five hundred people who probably *loved* white bread and Twinkies? It would be unforgettable, all right!

I was glad football season was over, so I could go straight home after school. I found Mom running on the treadmill.

"Yes, Pitt," she huffed, "I told Mr. Jordan I would be in charge of the supper. I hope I haven't bitten off more than I can chew." She slowed down to a walk and nibbled on a fingernail. "We can use the cafeteria ovens, so the potatoes will be a cinch, but what toppings should we serve? Let's see . . . yogurt, raw sunflower seeds—unsalted, of course—chopped broccoli, green peas, parsley, onions, green peppers, sesame seeds, wheat germ . . . "

"What about bacon bits? And sour cream and butter?" I suggested. "Maybe you should add them, too."

Mom's eyebrows almost jumped off her face. "Pitt! You know those are full of cholesterol and fat, not to mention preservatives! Now for dessert we could serve sliced apples." She looked uncertain. "Or maybe my Wheat Germ Delight . . . "

I was visualizing a football field under the lights of a hundred blazing ovens. Someone was running toward the wrong goal posts. Everyone was yelling, "Go back! Go back!" But it wasn't me carrying the ball. It was Mom.

I shook my head. "I tell you what, Mom. How about if you do the baked potatoes, and the band takes care of the toppings and the dessert? Then you won't have so much to worry about."

Mom's eyes lit up. "Why, Pitt, that's a wonderful idea!" I wasn't sure why I felt relieved. Now I had the ball!

I called Mr. Jordan right away and explained.

"Well, Pitt," he said, "I appreciate what you've told me, but do you think you kids can handle those details? This is the biggest project we've undertaken, and it sure is making me nervous." I could picture him snipping away at his mustache.

"Sure, Mr. Jordan. Food is really my specialty, you know. Trust me."

My strategy worked. It wasn't hard to get Mr. Benson to overrule Mom's superhealthy menu, and *nobody* argued with Mr. Benson.

It was unusually warm and breezy for December, I thought, as I helped set up the tables on Saturday. The aroma of hot baked potatoes filled the cafeteria, and our toppings—including sour cream, bacon bits, and butter—looked fresh and inviting. We had even gotten cherry pies donated for dessert.

Soon the line snaked all the way from the cafeteria, through the lobby, out the front door, and into the parking lot. The band cleared tables and brought drinks. My job was to make sure we didn't run out of anything on the potato bar.

"Didn't your mom say it would be an unforgettable experience, Pitt?" said Mr. Jordan, munching on a carrot. "You two make a good team in the kitchen."

"Thanks. But we don't really have the same philosophy about cooking," I called over my shoulder as I ran to pick up napkins that a gust of wind had blown off a table.

Then it hit. The doors banged closed and open again as the people in line rushed inside.

"Dust storm!" they shouted. The building rattled, and venetian blinds banged wildly. Lance and I ran to close the windows. Eaters caught with their mouths open crunched down on grit and pushed their plates away. Then the lights blew.

"Be calm! Stay where you are!" Mr. Jordan shouted over the uproar. Lance and I felt our way from window to window. By the time we finally got them all closed, the wind had dwindled but dust still hung in the air.

A few minutes later the lights came back on and we surveyed the damage. A layer of fine sand covered everything. Even Mr. Jordan's snowy mustache was cinnamon brown. There was nothing to do but refund dinner tickets and clean up. It was an unforgettable experience that we all wanted to forget.

Chapter 16

As the second semester wore on, Mr. Jordan became quieter and quieter. Nobody noticed it at first. After Christmas break, we were too busy running the concession stand at the basketball games. Then in February we started selling lemonade at tennis matches. And in the spring we began trimming hedges and hauling trash, holding bake sales, garage sales, car washes, anything that would help us reach our $40,000 goal. Mr. Jordan worked right beside us, his mustache dripping soap suds as he scrubbed windshields and shined bumpers.

Each Monday he filled in the big painted thermometer on the band-room wall. It was marked with figures at intervals—$5,000, $10,000, $15,000—all the way to $40,000, at the very top, in fluorescent purple and gold ink.

We had started off okay, Mr. Jordan happily filling it in almost to the $10,000 mark. Even Uncle Harley threw in $100 real money. Since then, though, despite our best efforts, the red paint in the thermometer was not climbing fast enough.

"Here it is the end of March," announced Mr. Jordan, "and we have only $26,000 in the bank, a little over half of what we need." He adjusted his glasses. "We have two months of school left to raise $14,000. If we can't do that, we'll have to forget the trip."

"Yes," Mr. Benson said. "The only event after school ends is the All-Region Track Meet in June, and that won't bring in much. You must meet your goal by May 30th, the last day of school."

Mr. Benson visited the band room a lot and was usually in a big hurry, just dumping stuff out of his briefcase onto Mr. Jordan's desk while he puffed on his cigar. One time though, he and Mr. Jordan talked for a long while in the office. I could hear snatches of conversation.

"Only way to go," from Melissa's dad, " . . . your last chance . . . "

" . . . I don't know . . . risky . . . " from Mr. Jordan. When they said good-bye Mr. Jordan looked more worried than ever, but Mr. Benson winked at us as he left.

"Pack your bags, kids!" he said.

I didn't know what Mr. Benson had in mind, but I decided to write someone who knew about reaching goals, someone who had started with nothing and become a big success—Jim Bob Smiley. He might be able to help me out in the girl department, too, I thought.

Though I don't usually like to write letters, that

night the words seemed to flow by themselves onto the paper.

Dear Jim Bob,

I bet you're surprised to get a letter from me. I hope you're not too busy, now that you're on TV, to give me some advice.

The problem is, we—that is the Desert Hills High School Band—need to raise $40,000 so we can march in the Independence Day Parade in Washington, D.C. Of course we're excited about it, but more than that, it would be a special going-away present for Mr. Jordan, our band director, in his last year. We've done everything you can think of—carnivals, potato suppers, car washes, house cleaning, garage sales, and concession stands. We need to come up with a really big money-maker and time is running out. Got any ideas?

Mom and Dad and Uncle Harley talk about you a lot, and Mom never misses your show. They want me to be like you—a real athlete, I mean. And Uncle Harley says with my genes I should be "Olympic Material". I wish it were true. Then maybe I'd stand a chance with Melissa—she's this girl I know.

Uncle Harley told me that that's the reason you started body-building—a girl, I mean. I hope you don't think I'm too nosy, but did it work? He told me about Charlotte and every-thing.

I'm working out with weights every day. I'm jogging and swimming and even eating my mom's cooking. Do you remember what that's like? Sometimes I fix my own food—not TV dinners, either. I've invented recipes for milk shakes, waffles, omelettes, tacos, and even birth-day cakes. It's really healthy stuff, too, made out of the same things Henrietta sells in her store. It tastes a lot better than what Mom cooks, but don't tell her that.

I'll stop now because I know you're very busy. I would appreciate it if you could help me think of a way to raise money. But if you can't, write to me anyway. I'd like to get a letter from you.

> *Thanks,*
> *Pitt*

The very next week Mr. Benson called a meeting of the band and the band parents to explain his last-ditch plan. Mr. Jordan stood by, snapping his scissors open and shut inside his pocket, as Mr. Benson mounted the podium.

"Ladies and gentlemen," he began. "We are in a difficult situation if we intend to get these young musicians to Washington. But don't be alarmed. I've been in difficult situations before and look at me now!"

Mom was looking at him, and she didn't approve of what she saw. "He shouldn't say that," she whispered to Dad. "He needs to lose at least thirty pounds!"

Mr. Benson continued. "Difficult situations call for daring solutions, and sometimes daring solutions require some risk."

"Uh-oh," said Dad.

" . . . So I have used my contacts in the entertainment world—and also $5,000 of the money we have raised—to contract with Noise, the most popular rock group this side of the Atlantic. They will perform at an outdoor concert on our football field April 25th."

Applause broke out from the band. "All right!" "Way to go, Mr. Benson!" He was an okay guy after all . . . in fact, he was a super guy! Most people I knew would kill for a ticket to a Noise concert. And they were going to play on *our* football field! I wouldn't need Jim Bob's help after all, at least for fund raising. Melissa was another story.

"You see," Mr. Benson continued, "Noise has a concert April 26th in Los Angeles, and it so happens that they were going to spend the night in Tucson anyway, only thirty miles from Desert Hills. So we are getting a special rate."

Uncle Harley stood up. "Five thousand dollars is a special rate?"

"Yes, sir," replied Mr. Benson firmly. "Now let me explain. If each band member sells fifty tickets, that will be 4,250 tickets sold. At $5.00 each, we will make $21,250. Add that to the $21,000 we have left after paying Noise and, you see, we will have $42,250—even more than we need."

But Uncle Harley wasn't satisfied. "Mr. Benson, you're giving the kids more tickets to sell than there are people in Desert Hills."

Mr. Benson smiled. "You're right. And that's why we're going to bus them to Tucson, so they can sell tickets there." Melissa's dad always seemed to have the answer.

Chapter 17

"Hurry up, Pitt!" Becky called as I walked into biology on Thursday. An acrid stench hit me at the door, like someone had thrown a burning match up my nose. That was when I remembered this was the day we were going to dissect frogs.

Becky and I had already picked out our frog and named him the week before. We put a little tag on him that said, "Gordo," because he was the fattest specimen in the lab—if you don't count Melinda Potts, that is. She sits at the next table.

I squeezed past Melinda and sat next to Becky. She was staring teary-eyed at Gordo, already in front of her in the wax-covered dissecting pan, looking like the main course of a cafeteria lunch. Beside the pan Becky had laid out our operating tools—some straight pins, a scalpel, a pair of forceps, and a couple of probes. Eight baby-food jars half-filled with a clear liquid were lined up behind.

"I don't feel well," Becky said.

"Gordo doesn't look so hot, either," I answered.

"No. I mean, I need some vitamin C." She sounded just like Mom.

Mr. Strohm, our biology teacher, rapped a pencil on the desk. We could hardly hear him over the squeals coming from the back of the class. Jimmy Watson had dropped his frog down Alice Warner's shirt.

"Ladies and gentlemen, your performance on this project will determine the major part of this nine-weeks grade." That got Mr. Strohm instant attention and absolute silence. "Now, let's get to work." He smacked his lips together. "Stretch the specimen on its back and fasten it in place with straight pins."

Becky was suddenly very busy getting a tissue out of her purse, so I turned Gordo over and pinned down his legs. I decided it hadn't been a very good idea to give him a name.

"Now pick up your scalpel and make an incision down the center of the frog," said Mr. Strohm. "Hold your scalpel loosely and stroke the tip of the blade along the skin."

Like an operating-room nurse, I slapped the scalpel into Becky's hand before she could protest. As she looked down at Gordo, the color drained from her face. I had to admire her though as she wiped her eyes with the back of her hand, gritted her teeth, and drew the scalpel down his belly. The skin pulled back like a released rubber band, and we had our first look at Gordo's grayish-pink insides. I whistled.

"Boy, he has guts!"

"Cut it out, Pitt."

"No, Becky," I laughed. "You're the one who's going to cut it out."

Becky gave me a fierce look as Mr. Strohm continued his instructions. She wiped her eyes again. I wasn't looking forward to this, either, but at least I wasn't crying. "You are to locate and remove the major organs with the probes and forceps," he said. "Place each in a separate jar of formalin and label it. Consult the diagram in your book to help you identify the body parts. Raise your hand for assistance."

Twenty hands shot up. "Not now!" commanded Mr. Strohm.

Becky and I started to work. "Heart," she pointed with the probe. I removed it with the forceps and put it in a jar.

"Lung . . . other lung . . . liver . . . " This project had already taught me one thing: I didn't want to be a surgeon.

"Stomach. . . . Hey, Pitt, what's that?"

I looked at the frog. I looked at the picture in the book. I looked at our labeled jars, but I couldn't figure out what it could be.

"That's weird," said Becky. "Look, it's right under his stomach."

"Hey, Becky, maybe Gordo has an exotic disease. We may have discovered something."

"Wait, Pitt. Let's look at it closer."

Mr. Strohm was way across the room, but I thought he should be in on this. I waved my hand in the air.

"Wait, Pitt!" whispered Becky.

There was a lot of talking in the room, so I had to yell. "Mr. Strohm! Hey, Mr. Strohm! Our frog has a tumor or something on his stomach."

Becky was pulling on my arm and telling me to shut up, but the whole class was already trailing Mr. Strohm to our table to look at Gordo's insides.

"Hm-m-m," he said, bending over what was left of Gordo. "Very interesting. Let's look with a magnifying glass." The kids jostled each other for a peek over his shoulder.

Mr. Strohm straightened up. "Just a moment, ladies and gentlemen." He picked up the forceps and poked around. The tumor seemed to be very thin. He clamped and lifted it for all of us to see. "Anyone lose a contact lens?"

Becky turned pinker than Gordo's insides. As she glared at me, the other contact swam down her cheek in a stream of tears and plopped into Gordo's open belly.

Chapter 18

"Washington, here we come!" I said to Uncle Harley the morning of the Noise concert. "We sold every ticket."

"That's great Pitt, m' boy! I couldn't be happier for you—or for Mr. Jordan." He laid a stack of mail on the table. "Guess I won't be there though. I don't need any more noise."

After he left I rummaged through the mail and found Jim Bob's letter at the bottom of the stack. My money worries were over, but maybe it would give me a clue as to how to use those 3,000 miles to make history out of Frank Schneider.

Dear Pitt,

So glad you wrote. It's hard for me to imagine you concerned about girls, since the last time I saw you, a wet diaper and a runny nose were your only concerns.

But to your question. Yes, for me body-building was the answer. Charlotte's in love with the new Jim Bob Smiley!

My best advice to you, however, is improve

yourself in all ways as you grow, but don't over-look those talents you already have. Remember it's impossible to make an apple out of a banana, but bananas are good, too.

By the way, I wrote to your uncle Harley. I believe he'll be able to help you with your fund raising.

All the best,
Jim Bob

It was hard to figure out what Jim Bob was talking about—apples, bananas, talents I already had? But it wasn't important now anyway.

Mom pushed open the door and dropped a big grocery sack labeled "Harv's Natural Foods" on the table. Panting, she began to unload it. She always jogged to Harv's and back.

"I've got to go help build the stage," I said.

"Okay, Pitt. What do you want for supper tonight?"

"A hamburger, fries, and a chocolate shake," I joked as I went out. Then something clicked in my head, like it does when I suddenly understand an algebra problem that I couldn't figure out before. Maybe I did have a special talent. I would have to discuss it with Uncle Harley sometime. I stuck my head back in the door. "Just kidding, Mom!" Then I got on my bike and headed for school.

It was eleven o'clock, and April felt like July. By

the time I got there, little salt rivers of sweat were running down my forehead and trickling into my eyes. I peeled off my shirt, wiped my eyes, and tied it around my waist. A stream of wolf whistles followed me as I trotted toward the football field. I felt pretty good about it until I saw who was whistling.

"Hey, Pitt!" Becky waved. She and Alex were practicing at the broad-jump pit. Now, would Jim Bob say they were apples or bananas?

"I've got to help set up the stage," I yelled, breaking into a run. A dozen kids were already hauling wood and hammering nails. I knew Melissa wouldn't be there though. She hated staying out in the sun.

Mr. Jordan gave me a high five as I climbed up on the platform. Perspiration dripped from the ends of his mustache, and his bald spot was beginning to glow like a neon sign, but he had never looked happier. "You're just in time, Kowalski! Here, finish this nail." He handed me the hammer.

"Ow!"

"Pitt, hammer the nail in the board, not the one on the end of your thumb!" By three o'clock the stage was ready for Noise.

"When will they be here, Mr. Jordan?" I asked as I helped him down.

"Who? The best rock group in the country? Mr. Benson will pick them up from the Tucson airport at five o'clock."

I had to laugh. Mr. Jordan didn't like heavy rock

any more than my parents did, but right now Noise was definitely his favorite band. He even hummed Noise's latest hit, "Armpits like Roses," as he drove away.

When I got back to school at seven o'clock, the stands were already half-full. I helped Lance take tickets. At 7:25 a niggling worry, like a night crawler, wriggled across my brain.

"Lance, have you ever gone to a rock concert?"

"Uh, no. Have you?"

"No. But I always thought it took them a while to set up the speakers and get the right sound balance and all that stuff."

"Sure," said Lance. "But I think they have somebody else do most of the work. They just check it and say if it's all right or something like that."

"Yeah," I said. "But where is the equipment? Why isn't somebody here setting it up?"

Lance shrugged. "Stop worrying, Pitt. I mean, this is Noise, man! It doesn't matter if they're a little bit late. Nobody's gonna leave. Just imagine, Noise at Desert Hills High!"

The stands buzzed with excitement, and groups of kids who'd missed out on tickets laughed and talked outside the fence. Every now and then one would try to sneak in with a group of people, but they were always caught.

The Desert Hills Police Department, which

consisted solely of Mac Watson, had recruited patrol-
men from Tucson to keep an eye on things. He
strolled importantly from one end of the stands to the
other with his thumbs hooked on the belt hidden
under his belly overhang.

"Say, wasn't this supposed to start at eight
o'clock?" he asked as he stopped by the gate for the
fifth time. "It's ten after."

Lance looked at his watch. "Yes, sir. They should
be here any time."

I spotted Mr. Jordan coming down from the
stands. The right side of his mustache was at least
one-quarter inch shorter than the left. That had to
have happened within the last half hour.

"Pitt, do you know Mr. Benson's home phone
number?" he asked. As a matter of fact, I did have it
memorized, but it wasn't because of Mr. Benson. I
wrote it down, and Mr. Jordan headed for the office.

My heart did a somersault every time a car pulled
into the parking lot. At 8:45 Mr. Benson still had not
arrived. The only noise was that coming from the
stands, where people were stomping their feet. Ten-
sion swirled through the crowd like a dust devil. . . .
And then Mr. Benson was at my elbow.

"Excuse me, boys." His face was very white
above the dark growth on his bulldog jowls. With a
sinking feeling in my stomach, I opened the gate and
let him pass.

He walked up the steps of the stage and stood at

the microphone. The crowd quieted as if someone had flipped a switch.

"Ladies and gentlemen, I have bad news," he began. "Noise will not be appearing tonight. I'm afraid they have been indefinitely delayed in Houston. . . . It seems they had a difference of opinion with the authorities there."

Chapter 19

"I tell you what," Mr. Jordan said to the band Monday morning. The look in his eyes didn't match his smile. "We'll have a great Fourth of July party right here in Desert Hills."

Everyone groaned. "Isn't there some way we can get the money we need?" asked Lance.

"Well," said Mr. Jordan, still hanging on to that determined smile. "The fact is that not only did we *not* earn the $21,150 we expected from the rock concert, but we also lost the $5,000 we paid as a booking fee. We may get it back someday, but certainly not in time for the trip." The smile dissolved into a long sigh. "So, unless someone can pull $19,000 out of a hat, there won't be any trip. We gave it our best shot, but . . . "

I didn't hear the rest. I was trying to remember what Jim Bob had told me. "Mr. Jordan," I interrupted, "don't give up yet. At least wait until the last day of school."

"Sure, Kowalski." Matt Henderson laughed.

Lance gave me a disgusted look. "Come on, Pitt. Be real."

Mr. Jordan tapped his baton for quiet. "All right, Kowalski. I won't cancel the motel reservations until June 1st. . . . Just in case a miracle happens."

The rest of my classes were a blur. *Just in case a miracle happens* kept running through my head. At 3:30 I hopped off the bus and ran to Uncle Harley's print shop.

"Yes, Pitt, m' boy, Jim Bob did write me about his idea," he said. "But I didn't think you would take it seriously."

"I am serious, Uncle Harley," I said. "Very serious."

Uncle Harley tugged his gold watch out of his pocket. "Then let's start planning. We have two and a half hours before dinner."

The planning was the easiest part. Actually doing it was something else again. What with running in the morning, working at the print shop after school, studying for finals, and lifting weights at night, I didn't even have time to think about Melissa.

"Aren't you going to the end-of-school dance?" asked Alex.

"No. Maybe I'll go out for dancing next year. I don't have time," I said. "Besides, who would I take? I suppose Melissa's going with Schneider."

"Well, you could take Becky."

I laughed. "As a matter of fact, I'm going to see if Becky will spend some time with me, but not dancing."

I needed Becky because she was as fast on the typewriter as she was on the track. It turned out she was willing to help me, but only on her terms. After two weeks, when we finally held the finished product in our hands, I was ready to celebrate. Instead, I found myself at the high school track during the hottest time of the day.

Becky squinted in the blinding afternoon sun. "How did you ever come up with enough recipes to make a cookbook, Pitt?"

"If you ate at my house, you'd have thought up at least that many, just to survive."

"But how did you do it, Pitt? I wouldn't know where to start."

"Well, Jim Bob gave me the idea. The hard part was testing the recipes to make sure they worked. Guess who's been doing all the cooking in our house!"

"What about paying for everything?"

"Uncle Harley says we'll take all the printing expenses out of the profit—if there is any. I just hope Jim Bob and Henrietta can sell them. We've only got two and a half weeks left before Mr. Jordan has to cancel our reservations."

"But $19,000, Pitt!"

"I know. But if you had seen Mr. Jordan's face when he gave all those people their money back at that concert . . . All I can do is try."

Becky leaned over and brushed an ant off my sneaker. "Well, I just want to tell you that I think it's neat you're doing this, Pitt, whether it works or not."

I didn't know what to say, so I said, "Thanks."

Becky jumped up. "Don't thank me," she answered. "We made a deal. I help you with the cookbooks, you help me get ready for the All-Region Track Meet."

How do I always get mixed up with sports nuts? I wondered. "Okay, Becky, when are you gonna run? I'm baking out here."

Becky stretched out and began to jog around the track. Naturally we were the only crazy people out at that time of day. It must have been 110 degrees, but Becky insisted she needed the track to herself.

I clicked the stopwatch on and off. My neck stung like it was too close to a hot stove, and I could feel freckles popping out like popcorn. Finally Becky stopped jogging and adjusted her white headband.

"I'm ready to run, Pitt. Say 'go' when you start the watch."

"Yeah, I know, I know," I assured her. "I'll say 'ready, set,' too."

Becky walked to the starting line and crouched. She dug her back foot around on the dirt, focused her eyes straight ahead, and waited.

"Ready . . . Set . . . Go!" I punched the watch as Becky pushed off, then watched, hypnotized by the rhythm of her stride. I had forgotten how fast she was.

Like a flash flood crashing down a dry riverbed, she rounded the curve, raced down the other side, and entered the stretch in front of me again. She whizzed across the finish line, broke to a trot, and finally walked back, panting hard, her face flushed, and damp hair clinging to the back of her neck.

"What's the time, Pitt?"

"What? Oh, about three o'clock."

"Pitt! Didn't you stop the watch?"

I looked down at the stopwatch, still ticking in my hand. "Uh-oh. Sorry, Becky. Run it again. I'll time you now, I promise."

Becky sighed and shook her head. "Can't. I'm pooped." She sat down beside me, resting her chin on her folded arms. "Just because you were so good at that, I'm gonna let you help me with the high jump."

"High jump?" I protested, wiping the sweat off my neck. "I thought you were pooped."

"Too pooped to run, but not to jump." Becky lifted her head and grinned at me. "How many books did we pack this morning, Pitt?" She gave me a jab in the ribs.

"Okay. Let's get to the jump pit before I'm baked, boiled, and fried."

I pulled extra foam pads into the pit. "How high do you want the bar?"

"Start at three feet for a warm-up." Becky took off, slow and steady, then faster and faster. Clearing the bar easily, she landed with a plop as Alex rode up on his bike.

"Sure that's not too high, Becky?" he teased.

She got up and brushed off her shorts. "Okay, you try it." They wouldn't stop jumping until at last I had a brainstorm.

"I'll buy you each a Coke." I never would have offered if I'd known who was at Sarah's.

Chapter 20

The blast of cold air as we walked into Sarah's felt like an arctic storm—just what I needed. Seeing Melissa cozied up to Frank Schneider was just what I didn't need.

"Let's sit here." I shouldered Becky into the nearest booth and slid in beside her with my back to Melissa.

"Hey, watch it!" Becky complained, slopping her Coke onto the table.

I hadn't noticed Linda sitting with Melissa and Frank, but she spotted us right away. "Alex! Alex! I'm over here."

She was at our table in nothing flat, her hands on her hips and the same expression on her face that I see on Mom's when I come in after curfew.

"I tried to call you all afternoon. Where were you?" she demanded, sliding into the booth beside Alex.

"I was, uh, practicing for the track meet with Pitt and Becky." He put his arm around her and gave her that magnetic smile.

"You told me you were going to study for finals all day."

Alex shrugged. "I needed to take a break." Then he pulled his arm down and faced her. "Anyway, I don't need to tell you every time I blow my nose."

Becky's knee nudged me under the table. I cleared my throat. Becky's knee whacked me so hard I thought I would land on the floor. "Hey, I just remembered. Becky and I need to go study for our biology final."

"You don't need to go anywhere, Pitt," Alex said with a tight smile.

Linda took his hand. "That's right, Pitt. Alex is coming over to our table anyway. We're going for a ride in Frank's car."

Alex sat like a rock. "I didn't say I was going anywhere."

Linda let go of his hand. Tears pooled in the corners of her eyes and began to trickle down both cheeks. She screwed up her face, and it looked like Hoover Dam had sprung a leak. "I just thought you'd like to," she wailed.

I swung my knees away from Becky, sure I was going to get bashed again, but Linda got up and started away.

Alex jumped up, all apologies. "I'm sorry, Linda. Sure, I'd like to go. Come on, don't cry."

We could hear the one-sided conversation all the way to the other table. Linda had decided she didn't want to go after all and sat pouting as Alex tried to make up.

Normally I would have moved to the other side of the booth, but since Melissa had to be looking our way, I slid closer to Becky and put my arm on the back of the booth behind her. Why not give Melissa some of her own medicine? Nothing else had worked.

I lowered my voice. "You're going to win the blue for sure in the 440, Becky, and probably in high jump, too."

Becky's eyebrows shot up. She wasn't used to getting compliments from me. "Do you really think so, Pitt? The jumping competitions always make me supernervous."

"Not with me there," I said, squeezing her shoulder. "I'm in charge of the high-jump pit this year. I'll be cheering for you."

Becky eyed me suspiciously. "Just make sure you have plenty of foam in there, Pitt. I want a soft landing! Once I've cleared the bar, I close my eyes so my contacts won't pop out and pray for a soft landing."

"Don't worry," I said. "I may not be so good at diagnosing frog tumors, but I'm great at jump pits."

Linda's protest drowned out Becky's answer. "No. I think I'll just go home!"

I turned around and sneaked a peek. "Come on, Linda," coaxed Melissa. "Frank will let you sit in the front. Won't you, Frank?"

"Uh, sure." When the four of them went out the door, Linda pointedly ignored Alex. She had that "serves-you-right" expression on her face. Alex looked resigned, and Frank just looked confused. The only smile I saw was on Melissa's face as she squeezed into the back with Alex.

Chapter 21

"Pitt! Pitt Kowalski!" It was Coach Fernandez. "I just want to shake your hand." Three of my fingers merged into one as he pumped my arm up and down. "Congratulations, boy! You are quite a businessman. Say, and look at those shoulders! What a change since September. We'll be looking for you in football next fall," he shouted as he hurried off. At last I knew how Alex felt when he saved the game.

"Hi, Pitt!"

"Good job, Pitt!"

Kids who'd never looked at me suddenly were my good friends. But the best thing of all was the smile on Mr. Jordan's face when I gave him that check on the last day of school.

"You did it, Pitt! You did it! How can I ever thank you? I'll just have to think of a way." Even his mustache curled up happily at the ends.

But I could always depend on Becky's treating me the same. She'd never let me forget how she helped that whole month of May. We'd studied for finals in between typing recipes. And while everybody else was at the end-of-school dance, we proofread the manuscript in Uncle Harley's print shop. Becky even left the athletic banquet early to help me finish.

A week after we sent the first 500 cookbooks, Jim Bob called from Detroit to order another 1,000 copies. He'd been plugging it on his TV show, and orders were flooding Henrietta's Health Food Store. We could hardly keep up. Uncle Harley refused to take any profit until we went over the top and the band had its $19,000.

I couldn't have done it without them. And I hate to admit it, but I guess I couldn't have done it without Becky either.

I kept my part of the bargain though. I'd been out on the track with her almost every day—timing, moving the high-jump bar, checking the pit. Now that All-Region Track Day was finally here, I was as nervous as she was.

"Hey, Pitt! Has Becky run yet?" It was Alex, with two gold medals and one silver swinging from his neck.

"Any minute," I answered. "Where's Linda? I thought she would come watch you."

"Changed her mind." Alex grinned. "The sun isn't good for her complexion, you know."

"I know." I had slathered myself with Sunblock-15 till I felt like a basted turkey. I was taking no chances on getting sunburned with the Washington trip just two days away.

"Finals—Girls' 440. Finals—Girls' 440. Take your

places at the starting line, please," the loudspeaker blared. Alex and I found a place toward the front of the crowd with a good view of the finish line.

Becky crouched in lane 3, licking her lips nervously. Suddenly my hands felt clammy.

"Ready . . . Set . . . Pow!"

Eight pairs of legs churned down the track, raising a cloud of dust behind them. Becky took the lead right off, but a tall Northside runner closed in on her. Becky lengthened her stride and pulled ahead.

"Man, she flies," breathed Alex.

"No kidding."

Becky glided down the track, a look of pure determination on her face. Her cheeks were flushed, and her bangs whipped above the white headband like dark wings over her face.

"She's beautiful when she runs." The look in Alex's eyes was respectful.

"Yeah. It's funny to think of Becky as beautiful," I said, almost to myself. "She's always been just . . . Becky."

Becky and two other girls, shoulders almost touching, pulled into the stretch. I couldn't tell who was ahead. "Come on, Becky! Come on, Becky!" My heart raced along with the pounding feet.

"Hi, Pitt!" A hand tapped my shoulder.

"Hi," I replied, following the runners with my eyes.

Then a light touch on my arm. "Pitt?"

I glanced around. "Oh. Hi, Melissa." I turned back to see Becky fall to third place. "Run, Becky!"

Melissa leaned around me. "I just wanted to say bye. We're moving back to Atlanta, you know."

"Moving?" I tried to look over her shoulder, but a tall boy had edged in front to block the view. "Why?"

Melissa was sunburned, and her eyes were red. Either she had a summer cold or she'd been crying. I noticed the skin on her nose was blistered leaving two big bubbles on the tip. "Oh, Daddy's business didn't do so well here." She looked at the ground. "I won't be going to Washington."

I felt bad for Melissa, but I didn't know how to tell her. Then cheering broke out from the stands. I yelled at Alex over the noise, "Who won?"

He shrugged his shoulders. "I couldn't see the finish. It was close."

The loudspeaker buzzed, then came to life. "Girls' 440: third place, Norma Wilson of Melville High; second place, Elena Sanchez of Northside High; first place, Becky Rivera of Desert Hills!"

"She did it! She did it!" I took Melissa's hand. "I wish you the best, Melissa, I really do. Sorry, would you excuse me?" I pushed through the crowd and ran toward the finish line.

Becky was in the middle of her teammates, who were yelling and hugging and patting her on the back.

"Hey, give *me* a chance!" I plowed through the

mob. A handshake didn't seem enough, so I gave her a big hug.

"Pitt, I'm so sweaty!" She laughed. "Besides, you're cracking my ribs."

"You're just right, and how could I crack your ribs with my marshmallow muscles?" It felt so good, I wanted to go on hugging her. But she pushed me off.

"Pitt, here come Melissa and Alex."

Alex had his arm around Melissa's shoulders, and she looked happy and sad at the same time. They didn't even look at us as they walked by.

"Well, what do you know!" I exclaimed.

"Do you care?" asked Becky, looking at me out of the corner of her eye.

I looked at Becky then—really looked at her. "No, I don't care," I answered, with a smile meant just for her.

The loudspeaker crackled. "All participants and officials for girls' high-jump report to the high-jump pit."

"That's me," said Becky.

"Me, too. Come on." I put my arm around her as we walked across the field.

"Good luck, Becky. You know you can do it."

"Let's pull those foam pads to the middle," the official said to me. "Okay, girls, line up for your practice jumps."

Again and again, higher and higher, Becky hurled herself over, head and shoulders first, arching backward, and finally kicking out her feet to clear the bar. It didn't take long to eliminate all but her and one other contestant.

I raised the bar one more time. "Five feet, one inch," announced the official.

Becky fixed her eyes on the bar and pushed off deliberately, measuring each step, then picked up speed and sprang into the air. . . .

Chapter 22

Plenty of time for writing anyway, I thought miserably, as I licked and sealed a letter to Jim Bob. I could hear firecrackers popping in the distance. Outside, the sun's rays were already turning the sidewalks into griddles. This was going to be the kind of day the *Gazette* carried pictures of people frying eggs on their cars—a typical Fourth of July in Arizona.

I bet it was hot in Washington, D.C., too. The kids in the band were probably putting their uniforms on. I should have been there on that crowded Washington street instead of here in this boring hospital room. I fingered the two shiny gold medals that hung on a vase of red carnations. At least Becky had won her events.

"Pitt? Pitt, can I come in?" Big brown eyes peeked around the corner.

"Becky!"

"Hey, Pitt, how are you?" She sat down gingerly on the edge of the bed and set a paper bag on the counter by the sink.

"Not so great . . . That is, till you came." I eyed the sack. "What'd you bring me?"

"Greedy, aren't you? It's just a box of brownies . . . and this." She opened the sack and took out the *Desert Hills Gazette.*

"Thanks, Becky, but I think you'd better find a hiding place for the brownies. You know how my mom feels about chocolate."

"But these are Carob-Honey Brownies from that famous cookbook, *150 Ways To Make Healthy Food Look And Taste Like Real Junk Food!* Speaking of which . . . " She unfolded the newspaper, and there on the front page was a picture of me holding my book in one hand and giving a check to Mr. Jordan with the other.

"Mr. Jordan had them wait until the special Fourth of July edition to publish this, Pitt. He thought you'd like that."

The caption read, "Local high school boy strikes it rich, sends Desert Hills Band to Washington, D.C." Under the picture was a two-column article. Becky shoved the paper into my hands.

Pitt Kowalski, son of Tom and Judith Kowalski of Heaven Hill Trailer Park, besides being a talented young chef, has proven himself to be innovative when it comes to making money, and unselfish when it comes to sharing that money. A member of the Desert Hills H.S. Marching Band, Pitt was actively involved in raising the needed $40,000 to send the band to Washington,

D.C. to participate in the Independence Day Parade. Due to unfortunate circumstances, notes Mr. Eugene Jordan, band director, the band was still short $19,000 as the school year ended. He was on the verge of canceling the trip when he was presented a check for the needed amount by Kowalski.

Pitt, whose parents are noted sports and health-food enthusiasts, created, tested, and compiled 150 recipes into a unique volume called 150 Ways To Make Healthy Food Look And Taste Like Real Junk Food. The book was printed and bound with the help of his uncle, Harley Kowalski of Kowalski's Print Shop. Principal distributors of the book have been Jim Bob Smiley, host of the nationally televised physical-fitness program "Jump with Jim Bob," and Henrietta Hawthorne, proprietor of Henrietta's Health Food Store in Detroit, Michigan. The book is also available locally through Kowalski's Print Shop of Desert Hills.

I put down the paper and tried one of Becky's brownies. "It's good they took that picture before the track meet. Can you imagine me on the front page with this cast propped up in the air?"

"Yeah." Becky brushed crumbs off my chin. "I feel bad about your missing the trip to Washington. It isn't fair when you're the one who raised all that money."

"With your help," I interrupted. "Besides, it wasn't your fault. I shouldn't have decided to adjust the foam in the pit right then."

"But I shouldn't have made such a big deal about having a soft landing. As it turned out, landing on you wasn't so soft anyway!"

"But I can't figure out," I said, "how you just got a bruise and I got a broken leg. You'd think it would've been the other way around."

Becky grinned. "Shows you who's tougher."

"I'll show you who's tougher." I grabbed her two hands.

"Pitt Kowalski, stop that!" boomed a voice from the door. It couldn't be anyone but Uncle Harley, who carried three newspapers under his massive arm.

"Seen this yet?" he asked, unrolling all three at once to reveal three me's with three glinting smiles and three cookbooks.

"Yes, Uncle Harley, Becky brought me a paper already."

Uncle Harley eased himself into the green chrome-and-plastic chair in the corner of the room and clicked his teeth together in happiness. "Did you see my name in there? By golly, they spelled it right, too! Now that's really something!" He looked up from the paper. "Becky, how are you? Why, your name should have been in there, too, the way you helped Pitt every day."

"No," answered Becky. "Pitt was helping me every day, too, with my running and jumping." She looked at my bare toes peeking out from the cast. "In fact, I think he helped me a little too much!"

Uncle Harley's bushy eyebrows furrowed into a V over his nose. "Yes, it's a shame about the trip, Pitt, m' boy. But at least you can watch it on television. Say, when does the parade start?"

"In only five minutes," Dad said from the door as he and Mom walked in. "Thought we'd keep you company, son."

All smiles, Mom came to the other side of the bed and gave me a noisy kiss. She had gotten all mushy when she saw that the cookbook was dedicated to her, and it still hadn't worn off. She checked her watch. "Turn on the TV, Pitt."

I pushed the button on the remote control. Sound crackled from the set, and a picture appeared on the screen, a quiz show. I changed channels until a crowded street scene came into view. The camera panned through the throngs of people to the reviewing stand. Even the President was there.

After reeling off names of the dignitaries who were present, the commentator interrupted himself. "Ladies and gentlemen, for those of you who just tuned in, welcome to the annual Independence Day Celebration from the nation's capital. Thousands have gathered here this morning along Pennsylvania Avenue to view the parade. It's a real scorcher, but the heat isn't diminishing the enthusiasm of the young musicians taking part today. You will see fifty high school bands, representing each state in the union, as well as . . . "

"Oh, Pitt." Mom pulled a plain white envelope from her purse. "This came in yesterday's mail." Opening the letter, I recognized Jim Bob's scrawl immediately.

Dear Pitt,

Your parents called with news of your accident. Here's hoping those size 13s are up and running soon.

Henrietta is still selling your book like hot cakes, whole-wheat hot cakes, that is. You may have to send her more copies soon.

This is the last letter I'll be writing from Detroit. When you write back, address the letter to: Jim Bob Smiley, General Delivery, Hogsbreath, Arkansas. Why, you ask? Well, I've spent fifteen years trying to be an apple when all the time I was a banana!

Our correspondence has helped me discover that the most important thing is to be what you are and do what you do best. So that's why I'm heading south. There's a little farm and some pigs waiting for me there.

Charlotte? I've told her of my decision. Now she'll have to make her own.

Best regards,
Jim Bob

As I reached the last line, Uncle Harley sat up in his chair. "The parade's starting!" he announced.

We watched as band after band passed the reviewing stand, an Uncle Sam on stilts saluted the crowd, and red, white, and blue floats glided by.

"Here comes Desert Hills!" Dad said. Becky squeezed my hand.

Sure enough, the purple and gold banner flapped proudly in the air—DESERT HILLS HIGH SCHOOL, DESERT HILLS, ARIZONA. A shiver of pride ran down my spine.

Becky leaned forward. "What's on the trombones?"

The band stopped in front of the reviewing stand, and the TV camera zoomed in on the front line of trombones. Fluttering in the wind, dancing back and forth with the music, on the slide of every trombone were tied purple and gold ribbons!

Pack your bags for fun and adventure with

SLEEPOVER FRIENDS™

by Susan Saunders